LEATHERBACK
BLUES

THE WILD PLACE ADVENTURE SERIES

Howl
The Truth About Brave
Saving Crazy

The Wild Place
Adventure Series

LEATHERBACK BLUES

By KAREN HOOD-CADDY

DUNDURN
TORONTO

Cover Images: istockphoto.com/yoyoyai; shutterstock.com/Maquiladora; 123rf.com/ioannaalexa
Printer: Webcom

Library and Archives Canada Cataloguing in Publication

Hood-Caddy, Karen, 1948-, author
    Leatherback blues / Karen Hood-Caddy.

(The wild place adventure series)
Issued in print and electronic formats.
ISBN 978-1-4597-4017-4 (softcover).--ISBN 978-1-4597-4018-1 (PDF).--
ISBN 978-1-4597-4019-8 (EPUB)

    I. Title. II. Series: Hood-Caddy, Karen, 1948- . Wild place
adventure series.

PS8565.O6514L43 2018   jC813'.54   C2017-905726-X
                                                 C2017-905727-8

1 2 3 4 5   22 21 20 19 18

We acknowledge the support of the **Canada Council for the Arts**, which last year invested $153 million to bring the arts to Canadians throughout the country, and the **Ontario Arts Council** for our publishing program. We also acknowledge the financial support of the **Government of Ontario**, through the **Ontario Book Publishing Tax Credit** and the **Ontario Media Development Corporation**, and the **Government of Canada**.

Nous remercions le **Conseil des arts du Canada** de son soutien. L'an dernier, le Conseil a investi 153 millions de dollars pour mettre de l'art dans la vie des Canadiennes et des Canadiens de tout le pays.

Care has been taken to trace the ownership of copyright material used in this book. The author and the publisher welcome any information enabling them to rectify any references or credits in subsequent editions.

— *J. Kirk Howard, President*

The publisher is not responsible for websites or their content unless they are owned by the publisher.

Printed and bound in Canada.

VISIT US AT

dundurn.com | @dundurnpress | dundurnpress | dundurnpress

Dundurn
3 Church Street, Suite 500
Toronto, Ontario, Canada
M5E 1M2

To Maggie Monteith,
a kindred spirit

Behold the turtle. He makes progress only when he sticks his neck out.
— James Bryant Conant

PROLOGUE

The men chased her. Dark figures in the dark night. She dug her toes into the gritty sand to get traction, but her feet sank into the beach's cement-like wetness. Afraid, violently afraid, she hurled herself forward, staggering to get her balance. Run. RUN!

Feet thudded behind her. She heard the see-saw sound of grabbed-for breath. Close. Then closer. She pumped her legs up and down and up and down, over and over. A hand clenched her arm.

Fiercely, she yanked herself free, but the force of the movement pitched her forward. She buckled, then smashed down hard on the sand. Blood burst from her lower lip. She scrambled up, but the men had her now. Gripping her arms, they hauled her into the air, kicking legs and all, and carried her to a van in the bushes. They threw her inside, gagged her, and bound her hands and feet.

Frantic with fear, she lay in a tight ball, her heart pounding like a fist against a brick wall.

CHAPTER ONE

THREE MONTHS EARLIER

The phone rang and rang. Robin wiped the last bit of grunge from the metal cage, dragged one soapy hand along her jeans, and reached for the phone.

"The Wild Place Animal Shelter." She felt excited. This was the first call of the season.

"You take raccoons?" a man growled. "Baby ones? I got three. Half-dead."

Robin's stomach clenched. *Half-dead?* Why? Where was the mother?

"Can you bring them in to the shelter?"

"Don't drive."

Robin turned to her grandmother, who was cleaning cages beside her.

"Griff, can we do a pickup? Three baby raccoons." She put her hand over the mouthpiece. "Half-dead, the guy said."

Griff nodded and started to untie the apron she always wore in the barn, the one with a huge owl on the front. "We better get a move on then." She pushed her long braid of silvery-white hair over her shoulder.

"Be there as soon as we can." Robin scribbled down directions and hung up.

Zo-Zo, her best friend, walked across the barn carrying a stack of cages.

"Half-dead's better than three-quarters dead," Zo-Zo said. She set the cages down and pushed her thick glasses that were as big as swim goggles farther up her nose. "Remember that loon last year? He looked as dead as a doornail when he came in. But he lived."

Yeah. Robin smiled. She'd thought he was a goner too. She winced, remembering. Some kid had hit him with his boat. The loon had bruises on every part of his body. She'd had to work her heart out, but she had saved him. Her reward had come a few months later, when they'd been able to release him and she'd watched him fly off into the wild blue sky. If only all rescues could end so well.

Zo-Zo tightened the laces on her flame-red sneakers. "How many baby raccoons are we picking up?"

"Three."

"What happened to the mom?"

Robin shrugged. She should have asked. What was the matter with her?

She yanked off her barn shirt. It was one of her dad's old plaid ones, big enough to go over her regular clothes. Every time she wore it, she felt as if she was being hugged by him.

"Meet you in the van."

She walked quickly to the farmhouse and went into the kitchen. It smelled of the toast they'd had there a little while ago. Zo-Zo had stayed over and they'd made

French toast, thick and fluffy, then slathered chunky bits of butter on top and a ton of maple syrup. Her brother, Squirm, had eaten five pieces.

She checked the coat rack. Her dad's coat was gone. He must have already left for the vet clinic. But Ari's over-the-knee leather boots were there. They were tall and elegant. Like something out of a fashion magazine.

Robin yelled up the stairwell.

"Ari!"

Silence yawned into the space. Robin dashed up the stairs and burst into their shared bedroom. Her sister was sitting on the bed, painting her toenails. She looked up at Robin with a pained expression and pulled one side of her headphones slightly away from her ear. There was the sound of pounding music.

"We're going on a rescue. Can you listen for the phone?"

Ari stared at her as if Robin had just asked her to wash the floor.

Robin stared back. Why did she have to have such a girlie-girl sister? Why couldn't she have a sister who loved the shelter like Zo-Zo did?

The word *half-dead* repeated in her mind. She spun around and hurried down the stairs. The time between half-dead and full-out dead could be short. She knew that from experience. There was no time to waste.

When she got to the van, she unzipped the big maroon rescue bag and checked the contents: blanket, shovel, scissors, two knives, a sling, various lengths of rope, packages of formula, water, bandages, antiseptic creams, and other medications. Everything was there.

"Come on," Zo-Zo called from the front seat.

Robin left the bag unzipped, pushed it forward, and climbed into the back. She was about to shut the door when Relentless jumped in behind her, her dog eyes pleading, *Let me come this time, PLEASE?*

Robin ran her open palm over her dog's sleek, black forehead. She used to take Relentless on rescues, but a drunk hunter had taken a shot at her last year, so Robin left her at home now. Rescues could be dangerous. And there was something about this one that was feeling weird.

"You'll get your chance to help later," Robin said and eased Relentless out of the van.

Griff climbed into the driver's seat, smiled at Zo-Zo, and started the engine. They were pulling away when the back door of the van sprang open. In a dramatic, commando-style manoeuvre, Squirm threw himself in beside her.

Robin rolled her eyes upward. "Oh, Squirm." When was this Ninja Turtle stage ever going to end?

Squirm began juggling jujubes. "Where we going?"

"You'll see." Squirm was eleven, two years younger, but he acted like he was the same age as her. With the same rights.

He caught one of the jujubes in his mouth, stuffed the others back in his pocket, and pulled open a tattered insect identification book that he kept in the side pocket of the van.

Robin glanced at the pictures of the brightly coloured insects. He had drawings and pictures like this all over his room too. The kids at school called him Bug Boy. The name fit him perfectly.

14

They careened down the driveway, then picked up speed on the main road. As usual, Griff drove the van like a fire truck on the way to a blaze. All that was missing was the siren.

Robin rolled down the window and stuck her head outside. She loved the spring. The air was dense and cool, but full of the smell of wet, moist things coming back to life. Finally. Only a few weeks ago the snow in the woods had been up to her armpits. But no more. Now it was gone. Completely gone. And the forest floor was dotted with yellow trout lilies and white trilliums. All her old friends were coming back — the purple crocuses, the yellow finches, the —

"Hey!" Robin shouted. The automatic window was sliding up, cutting into her throat. She groped for the window switch and pushed it hard. The window slid back down into the holster of the door.

She glared at Squirm. "What'd you do that for?"

Squirm thrust his bare, freckled arm into her face so she could see the goosebumps.

She looked him over. He wasn't wearing a jacket or much else to keep him warm. Only shorts and a T-shirt. Served him right if he was cold.

The van barrelled around a sharp corner and Squirm slid against her. When the van straightened, he stayed close, nestling into her warmth. She thought about pushing him away. It was his own fault that he had goosebumps. But feeling sorry for him, she reached back, pulled the blanket from the rescue bag, and wrapped it around him. Sometimes he was such a sucky puppy.

He fidgeted in his pocket and placed an orange jujube in her hand. Orange ones were his favourite. He didn't part with them easily.

Robin popped the jujube into her mouth. It exploded with flavour, like a little grenade. No wonder he liked them so much.

They drove on. She stared at Zo-Zo's hair, which was cascading over the back of the seat in front of her. Squirm reached forward and began tying some of the strands into knots. Robin swatted his hand away and untangled them.

"I wish I had hair like you," she said. It was so silky. But then, there were many things Zo-Zo had that she didn't. Great hair. Guts of steel. Too many other things to count.

Using a firecracker-red scrunchie, Zo-Zo scooped up her hair and tied it into a ponytail, just as she always did before a rescue.

Robin wished she could get her own hair out of the way like that. No matter how many clips and elastics she used, her corkscrew curls always found a way of springing lose. It was like having wild things living on your head. It was weird. Weirder than weird.

Squirm had curls too, but they were wavier. And orangier. Maybe that was from all the jujubes he ate.

Griff eyed Robin through the rear-view mirror. "People pay hairdressers big dollars for curls like yours. You got them from your mom."

Suddenly it was as if the van door had swung open and pitched Robin into a ditch. Why did Griff do this? Talk about her mother as if she were still alive?

Settle down, she told herself. *You can't go into a rescue if you're bent out of shape.*

The van slowed and pulled into a driveway. They parked in front of a three-storey red-brick house with a yellow porch. A man stood in front of the garage. He had white stubble on his cheeks and stood with his meaty arms crossed over his chest, elbows protruding.

Robin got out of the van with the others. It was her turn to take the lead, although she wasn't sure she was up to it. But what was the alternative? Being a wimp?

She reached into the rescue bag and pulled out a flashlight, rubber gloves, and a box to put the babies in. Hopefully they were still alive. *Please let them be alive.* She hated picking up dead animals. Especially baby animals.

Griff picked up another flashlight, reached for the blanket, and followed Robin as she walked toward the man.

The man pointed a yellowed finger at the roof of his house. "Must be a hole under the eaves," he said. "Saw the mother climb in but didn't know there were babies till I heard them mewing."

Robin stared into the man's watery eyes and made herself ask the question. "Where's the mother?"

The man fired his answer back at her. "Shot it."

Robin felt as if she'd been punched in the gut.

The man turned and walked toward the house.

Robin stood still, staring after him. Her throat burned with the hot, fiery words that wanted to come out. She wanted to shout at the man, scream at him for what he'd done, but she felt as if someone had tied a rope around her chest and was pulling it tight. It was all she could do to breathe. Her legs felt wobbly, as if they might collapse under her. Griff put her arm around Robin and edged her forward.

Stiffly, Robin took a step. "He shot the mother."

"At least he didn't shoot the babies," Griff said. "We have to give him credit for that."

I'm not giving him credit for anything. If the man had taken just one minute to peek into his attic, the baby raccoons would still have a mother.

Zo-Zo elbowed her and nodded to the right. Robin followed her friend's gaze. There, thrown on top of the garbage pail, was the mother's lifeless body.

In the middle of a step, Robin tripped and tumbled forward, almost smashing her face against one of the pillars on the porch.

"Take it easy," Griff said, reaching out to steady her.

Robin forced herself to take a deep breath. It wasn't good to start a rescue when she was all churned up like this. She had to calm down. But how? Her emotions were running wild inside her, and she felt like an inept teacher trying to control a rioting class.

They went inside and climbed the stairs. As they went, Robin listened to Griff and the man talk about the weather. *How could Griff do that?* The man was a murderer! He'd just *killed* a mother raccoon. Griff should be chewing him out big time. Why wasn't she? And why couldn't Robin say anything either?

They entered a bedroom and the old man led them to a closet. A stepladder was already set up inside. As Robin got near, she could smell the mustiness of the old clothes that were hanging there. He pushed them aside and pointed to a small, square hatch at the top of the cupboard.

Robin peered up at it. The hatch was small. Very small. *Uh-oh.*

The man stepped back. "I'll leave you to it."

Robin stared at the hatch. *What if I get stuck?* She made herself breathe and told herself not to make a big deal of it. *Just climb in, scoop up the babies, then get the heck out.*

She forced herself up the ladder and pushed her head through the hatch. The attic was dark. *Probably full of a million dead flies and spiders. And a million more live ones.*

"I need a flashlight."

Griff passed her one, and Robin fiddled with the settings. She was trying to buy herself some time. But there was no time to buy. She needed to get to the babies quickly and get them out.

Stop being such a wuss, she told herself.

Get moving!

The words sounded so loud, she thought she'd actually shouted them, but she hadn't.

"Go girl, go!" Zo-Zo called from below.

Robin could hear the urgency in Zo-Zo's voice.

Summoning all her will, Robin grabbed the sides of the hatch and wormed her shoulders and chest up into it. Her hands were slippery with sweat, and she could feel spiderwebs breaking against her face as she moved forward.

Her entire body was in the attic now. Heat, terrible heat, pressed against her, squeezing her lungs, making it hard to breathe. Was she going to faint? She wished now she'd let Zo-Zo climb in and not her. Zo-Zo wasn't a stupid wuss like she was.

She cast the light around the attic. Long wooden planks jutted up into a point at the top of the roof, and there were battens of pink insulation stuffed between them.

She scanned the room for raccoons. They were huddled in one of the far corners. Were they alive? They weren't moving, even with the blast of light hitting them. *What if they're dead?* If they were, she'd have to pull their limp bodies out. She'd have to touch them, she'd —

Oh, no. She was going to faint. She grabbed one of the joists to steady herself.

Griff poked her head up through the hatch. "Robin, are you all right?"

NO! Robin wanted to cry.

"Focus on the babies," Griff said. "The babies."

Robin made herself move. Her body cast gigantic shadows on the walls as she did. She inched toward the babies. Suddenly Zo-Zo appeared beside her. With fluid ease, she picked up one of the babies.

"It's alive!"

Zo-Zo's eyes were bright even in the dim light.

She handed one baby and then two others back to Griff.

"Come on," she said to Robin and scooted down the ladder.

Stiffly, Robin followed. When she stepped out of the closet, she almost bumped into Squirm, who was arranging the babies into a cardboard box.

Griff had her arm around Zo-Zo.

"Well done, girl."

Robin turned away, her face hot. Zo-Zo deserved the praise, but still. It would have been hers if she hadn't wimped out.

"Piece of cake," Zo-Zo said.

Robin's eyes widened. *Piece of cake? Really?*

"Let's get these little darlings back to the shelter," Griff said.

They all moved quickly to the van. Griff zoomed along the road while the three kids sat in the back and started to hydrate the babies.

Robin arranged one of the babies into the crook of her arm.

Please don't die. Please.

She positioned a needleless syringe filled with formula near its mouth. She let a little of the food spurt out so the baby could taste it, and sure enough, it opened its mouth and began to feed, making little snuffling noises.

Relief washed through her. But it was too early to let herself feel relief. She knew from experience that Death could come in a nanosecond and snatch any or all of these babies away. Death could take what it wanted, when it wanted. It was the cruellest thing ever. And she hated it.

She stared down at the baby raccoon. It was so tiny, not much bigger than a balled-up sock. It had the characteristic black mask around its eyes and rings on its tail. Its tiny ears were fringed white and its fingers were long and thin. She thought it was the most beautiful thing she'd ever seen. But then, she always thought that.

The raccoon continued to feed, and she felt herself start to relax. She didn't fight it now. The baby was taking in lots of food. It was going to be fine.

Robin reprimanded herself. She had to stop thinking the worst all the time. It was a bad habit. A bad habit she was going to have to break.

"How're they doing?" Griff called back to them.

Robin, who was sandwiched between Squirm and Zo-Zo, looked at the baby in her arms and the ones on either side of her. From what she could see, they all looked like they had enough life inside of them to keep going. But she'd thought that before. And had her hope ripped out of her.

Oh, stop.

Squirm chuckled. "My guy's guzzling the formula like there's no tomorrow. Think I'll call him Guzzler."

Zo-Zo piped up next. "Mine's got the prettiest little circles around her tail. I'm going to call her Ringer."

Robin let her head fall back against the seat. She shut her eyes. She was tired. The raccoon she was holding felt so peaceful. It had stopped feeding and wasn't moving or making any sound. It must have fallen asleep. Maybe she'd call it Sleepyhead or Snooze.

Her eyes snapped open as the realization hit her. She looked down at the baby raccoon. It was completely still.

Dead still.

CHAPTER TWO

Robin watched as Griff wrapped the baby raccoon in a blue tea towel, then laid it tenderly at the bottom of a wicker basket as if it were still alive. She passed the basket to Robin and they headed outside. Griff grabbed a small shovel as they walked past the barn. They skirted around Griff's cabin and followed a narrow path that wended its way through the shrubs and rocks along the shoreline.

It was just the two of them. Zo-Zo had gone home to have dinner with a visiting aunt, and Squirm and their dad were working on an insect project. Ari was at the library. Robin was glad to have Griff to herself for once. That didn't happen very often.

She glanced at the clearing up ahead. No one seemed to know why this small area had no trees. Except for a circle of old oaks that ringed the area like guardians, the land was as open as a meadow and covered with wild grasses and flowers. A large stump sat in the middle, as flat on top as a wooden table. The oaks usually shaded the area in the summer, but the trees hadn't leafed out yet and the sun was bright, so it was easy to see the dozen or so Popsicle sticks that marked the graves amongst the grasses. Each stick had a name and date written on it.

When they'd first started The Wild Place, there had been much discussion about what to do with the bodies of animals who died. Griff had suggested they bring the carcass of any such animal here to this secluded area and leave it on top of the tree stump.

Robin had protested. "But other animals will — they'll, they'll —" She couldn't bring herself to say the words.

"Eat it?" Griff asked, a smile playing on her mouth.

Squirm had made a face. "Gross."

"It's not gross at all," Griff argued. "It's the way of the wild. Animals are happy to give their bodies to other animals for food."

The kids had complained to their dad, and Gord had said, "Oh, Mom," as he sometimes did when Griff had gone too far.

Robin, backed by Squirm, had insisted that each and every animal was to have some sort of burial, so that's what they did. This morning was no exception.

Robin stood holding the lifeless body of the baby raccoon while Griff dug a hole. The animal, as small as it was, felt heavy in her hands. Robin felt heavy in her heart.

She stared into the hole Griff was digging. When it was deep enough, Robin eased the limp body of the raccoon into the cradle of earth. Griff knelt, and the two of them began to scoop the soil overtop.

Robin's eyes stung. She was burning with remorse. If she hadn't acted like such an idiot up in the attic, maybe this little raccoon would still be alive.

Griff pressed Robin's shoulder with her hand. It felt like a warm oven mitt.

"Remember, Robin, the raccoon might be dead, but its spirit is already flying free in the big Wild Place in the sky. Alongside your mother."

Robin liked thinking of her mother's spirit flying around. Sometimes she even imagined that her mother was close. When that happened, Robin felt ecstatic. But she always went away again. And Robin had to face the desolation of her being gone. Completely gone.

Griff continued. "So you don't need to be sad about the raccoon unless you want to."

Yeah, right. Robin sighed. Her grandmother made it sound like emotions were something you could chose to have or not have. It wasn't like that for her. Emotions came, took her over, and buzzed her up like food in a blender.

Griff leaned her back against a wide tree trunk and closed her eyes. Her face was soft with serenity. "It's so peaceful here."

Robin swallowed hard. Being in a blender wasn't peaceful. No way.

Griff scrutinized her face. "Are you still fussing about what happened up in that attic?"

Robin didn't know what to say. She opened her mouth to speak, but nothing she could say would make what she'd done all right.

Griff shook her head. "A lot of people are uncomfortable in closed-in spaces. They're not my cup of tea either."

"I thought I was going to faint," Robin said.

"You got scared. It happens."

"Not to Zo-Zo! She *never* gets scared."

Griff whisked an ant off her slacks. "Zo-Zo may not show it, but I bet she gets afraid sometimes too. Everybody does. The world is scary sometimes. So stop telling yourself you shouldn't be afraid. It's a waste of time. Accept your fear and move on."

Robin dropped her head in despair. She didn't want to accept her fear. She wanted not to have it.

"I wish I wasn't such a wuss."

A wounded look came over Griff's face. "You, a wuss? You're one of the bravest people I know."

Robin stared at Griff doubtfully.

"Remember that day the sheriff came to take away the animals? Before we had our licence? You chained yourself to the barn and wouldn't let them in." Griff put her hand over her mouth. "I shouldn't be smiling, but I don't think I've ever been so proud ..."

"Proud? You and Dad grounded me for like a year!"

"It wasn't a year. Maybe a few weeks but — we had to do something. After all, you *were* breaking the law."

Adults. They were so confusing.

"And what about that campaign you did to stop factory farming? You stood up to the whole town. Same way you stood up to the whalers in the Antarctic. That took guts."

Robin swallowed. Griff was exaggerating. "But I was afraid a lot of the time ..."

"Of course you were afraid. You were doing afraid-making things. That's what courage is: being afraid and doing something anyway."

"I want to be like Zo-Zo. And not be scared at all."

"You're not Zo-Zo. You need to trust yourself and do things in your own way. You've had some tough things happen. Not many kids have to face the loss of a parent. That's big. Enough to make anyone a little nervous about life."

Big, Robin repeated in her head. It was such a little word. A mere drop of water in a tsunami of feelings that she'd never be able to express.

Griff picked up an acorn and rolled it between her fingers. "I think you were brave for even attempting to go up into that attic. It was so hot."

"Zo-Zo loves the heat," Robin said. "It was just so claustro — claustro —"

"Claustrophobic?"

Robin nodded. "I couldn't handle it. I froze, I —"

"You were just taking a minute to gather yourself, Robin. If Zo-Zo hadn't charged up there, you would have gotten your bearings and carried on."

Robin wasn't convinced. "If it hadn't been for her, *all* the raccoons might have died, instead of just one." The tears began to gush out of her.

Griff pulled Robin into her arms, enveloping Robin's small body in her large one. Robin wanted to struggle, but the warmth of her grandmother and the fierce love that powered it made her surrender.

Griff stroked her forehead and hair.

When Robin had stopped crying, Griff opened Robin's hand and placed the acorn in the middle of her palm.

"Do you think this acorn knows it has the makings of a gigantic oak tree?" She looked at Robin. "I doubt it." She shook her head. "I think you have the makings of becoming an amazing environmentalist."

Robin closed her eyes. Griff was going too far. Way too far.

"You'll see," Griff said. "But to do that, you're going to have to believe in yourself. Even when you're afraid."

Robin examined the acorn. It was a big one, smooth and round on the bottom with a kind of thatched hat on the top.

"Can you feel the energy inside it?" Griff asked.

Robin closed her eyes. She could feel a very slight thrumming. As if there was something inside the acorn that was just bursting to get out.

"That's like you," Griff said. "You have all these feelings that you're trying to handle. And when you do, look out, world! You're going to make a difference. You'll see."

What Griff was saying was crazy! Crazy! But Robin tucked the acorn in her pocket anyway. She wanted to keep it close.

CHAPTER
THREE

It was just past dawn when Robin heard a vehicle. She could hear tires crunching on the stones in the driveway, then brakes squealing. Doors opening and closing.

Oh, no!

She yearned to roll over and sink back into the warm arms of sleep, but she couldn't. She knew what those sounds meant. Reluctantly, she yanked back the quilt and sat up.

She pulled a fleece over her cotton pajama top, stuffed her legs into some jeans, and thumped the lump under the covers at the bottom of the bed. Relentless groaned, but oozed herself out from between the sheets as Robin pulled on some bright-green Crocs. In the other bed, Ari snored lightly.

By the time she'd rushed downstairs and pulled open the front door, all she could see of the car was its tail lights pulling away. A large box sat in the middle of the driveway. No air holes had been punched into the cardboard. An animal of some sort was in there, that was certain. What wasn't certain was whether or not it would be alive.

Probably not, if the person driving had come a long way. One time someone had dropped off a box with a finch inside and left it in the blazing sun. Robin and everyone else had been in town. By the time they got back to attend to it, the bird was lying on its back, its stick-thin legs pointing up into the air.

Quietly, she stepped toward the box and slowly, very slowly, lifted the lid. A porcupine! It stiffened, its quills rising into firing position. She reared back, grabbing her dog's collar. Porcupines couldn't shoot their quills, but if Relentless pushed her snout in close enough for contact, she'd get dozens of needle-sharp quills fired into her face. Robin had helped her dad pull quills out of Relentless on three occasions now, yanking each one out with a pair of pliers as her dog yelped. She didn't want to start her day with a chore like that.

She was just about to shut the lid and take the box inside when she saw something red smeared on the card-board. Blood? She took a closer look at the animal, moving around the box so she could see it from various angles. It was hard to see beneath the animal's protective coat of quills, but when she stood right in front of it, she could see a nasty-looking bruise just above its eye. Outrage exploded inside her. Who had done that? And why?

Keeping one hand firmly on her dog, she used the other to close the box, then ran inside and up the stairs. She put Relentless in her bedroom and scurried down the hall to her dad's room.

She tapped quickly on the door and entered the dim bedroom. Her father was sleeping, curled up on one side of the bed. The same side he'd always slept on when her mother was alive. The other half of the bed was empty. A wave of sadness washed over her, but she managed to push it away and speak.

"Dad," she whispered. "Dad! There's a 'D and D' in the driveway." Griff had coined the phrase years ago. It stood for "drop and dash." People did D and D's when they wanted to get rid of an animal or they had hurt it and didn't want to be identified.

He jerked up. "How bad?"

"I'm not sure. It's a porcupine. It's got a gash on its face —"

"Be right there," he said.

Robin ran back down the stairs and out to the barn. She pulled on some rubber gloves and cleaned the surgery table with some antiseptic. It had a strong medical smell and made her sneeze.

Around her, the cupboards were full of all the veterinary gear and supplies needed to treat the various health issues they encountered at the shelter. Robin loved this room. It was where she got to see her father work. Often, when he was doing what he called "nuts and bolts" stuff, like stitching up cuts and setting bones, he'd let her pass him instruments or ointments, which she found thrilling. On a few occasions, she'd helped save an animal's life. Nothing was better than that. Nothing.

Robin grabbed an intake form and began filling it out. She wasn't sure what to put in the box that said "approximate age." So many of the animals they took in at this time of year were babies, and this one was no exception.

Babies always seemed to be getting into trouble. Maybe it was because they were so new to the world and just didn't know how things worked, but they were always getting their feet caught in fishing lines, or falling out of nests, or squeezing themselves into places they couldn't get out of. If a baby animal could get itself into a mess, it would.

When her dad came in, he looked rumpled but awake. He took a sip of coffee, then got to work administering some anaesthetic. The moment he did, the porcupine slumped into a drug-induced sleep.

Now that they didn't have to worry about quills, they lifted the porcupine onto the scales.

"Ten kilograms," she said and wrote that on the form.

She watched as her father did his examination. The porcupine had a stocky body, like most porcupines, and a small face. Black and white quills, some as long as ten centimetres, cascaded down its back, some trailing onto the table.

Robin reached out and let the tip of her finger touch the end of one of the quills. *Sharp.* She withdrew her hand and watched as her father dabbed some ointment on the bruise.

"Someone must have thrown a rock at it or something," he said.

Robin felt herself tense.

"Why?"

The word punched the air between them like a fist. She didn't mean to say it so strongly, but she couldn't always control herself. It just made her so *mad* the way people treated animals.

Her father arched an eyebrow but smiled wryly. "Who knows? Maybe they were trying to stop it from quilling their dog. Given that each porcupine has a personal arsenal of at least thirty thousand quills, that can be quite a concern." He added more ointment to the wound. "As you and I know from experience. How many quills did we pull out of Relentless the last time she attempted to cozy up to a porcupine?"

Robin shrugged. She could have told him: 154. She had the quills in a bottle that was somewhere in this very room. But for some reason, she didn't want to tell him. His cheeriness was bugging her. She didn't feel like being cheery.

Her father gave the porcupine a shot of antibiotics.

"A few days of R and R and we'll be able to release this guy back to the wild."

Over the years, they'd released every kind of animal — mostly raccoons, porcupines, and skunks, but there had also been herons, hummingbirds, squirrels, bears, and deer. Releasing animals was the best part of running a wild animal shelter. Usually, even the idea of it filled her with happiness. But not today.

She levelled her gaze at her father. "Don't you ever get mad at the way people treat animals?"

"Of course I do," he said, looking a bit miffed. "But there will always be good and bad things in the world. Things that are complete opposites. Night versus day. Black versus white. It's the way things are."

Robin frowned. She hated it when he did his "The Way Things Are" lecture.

He continued. "Which means you get to choose which side you want to be on."

It didn't feel like a choice. She was on the side of the animals. And the environment. What scared her was that so many people weren't. It made no sense to her. The earth was *home*. The animals were the *family* in that home. No one should be fouling up their home. Or hurting their family. It scared her that people were willing to do that.

"So, what am I supposed to do? Just accept bad things? Just yawn and say, 'Oh well, *whatever*!'"

He gave her his *you know I don't mean that* look.

"I just don't want you getting upset all the time. I want you to learn to control your emotions."

HOW? she wanted to shout. Griff and Gord made it look so easy, but it wasn't. At least not for her. Every time she saw an animal being mistreated, or heard about another oil spill, the injustice of it fired her right up. Even when she didn't want to be fired up. Other kids didn't get upset like she did over environmental stuff. How come she was so different? It was as if she belonged to another species. It was like being neon green when everyone else was brown. She didn't fit. And never would.

She thrust her hands deep into the pockets of her shorts. Her fingers found the acorn Griff had given her. She rubbed her fingers against its belly-like roundness. It was soothing somehow. The faint thrumming she'd felt the other day was still there. What was that thrumming? The force that would make it a giant oak tree one day? Was that the same force that was in other living things? Even her?

Her father looked at her with kind eyes.

She let out a long breath of air. "I just don't know how to settle myself down sometimes."

"You and everyone else your age," he said and smiled.

She sighed. "It's good that we patch up these animals and send them back into the wild, it's just that I want —" Dare she say it? "I just want to do something bigger."

"Be careful what you ask for," he said. "You very often get it."

Griff cracked open the door and poked her head in. "Some baby skunks just came in," she said. "A man found them on the road."

"Be right there," Gord said.

"I'll go mix up some formula," Griff said. Behind her, the phone rang again and she went off to answer it, calling behind her, "They're in the kitchen where it's warm."

Robin and her father lifted the sleeping body of the porcupine into a large cage and then walked over to the farmhouse. To another cardboard box. Was this her life now, moving from one cardboard box to another?

She opened the flap of the box and saw the two baby skunks. All her angst evaporated. Gord sipped his coffee, then picked up his stethoscope and began to examine the baby skunks. Robin studied his face as he looked them over. He might assess an animal's health from the symptoms he saw, but she did the same just from looking at his brow. One worry line meant *all is well*, two worry lines meant *better keep on eye on this one*, and three meant *go get the shovel — we'll be burying this one soon*.

This time there was only one worry line — the skunks would live.

"Ew, skunks," Ari said, coming into the kitchen. She was wearing pink sneakers, a pink top, and tight white jeans. Robin hated pink. It was a stupid colour that only girlie-type girls like Ari would wear.

"Can you drive me to the library, Dad?"

Library! Ha! Robin thought. The library was Ari's favourite excuse for going into town and seeing her friends.

"Sure, just help us finish feeding these skunks," he said.

Ari recoiled. "No way. Skunks spray!"

"Not baby skunks," Squirm said. "Everybody knows that!"

Griff came in, carrying a container of formula in one hand and a pile of mail in the other. She tossed the mail on the table and slumped down in a chair. "I need a cup of tea, and I need it now."

"Can *you* drive me to the library?" Ari asked her.

"No, but Zo-Zo and her dad just pulled up," Griff said. "If you're quick, he can take you. It's right on his way."

Ari ran outside, and Zo-Zo ran in just as the phone rang. Without a word, Zo-Zo took the baby skunk Gord was holding so he could get the phone. She knew the routine.

Griff made herself a cup of tea and looked through the mail.

"Oh, good, there's one from Finn."

"Say hi to him when you write back," Robin said. They'd gone with Finn to Antarctica last year to save whales, and it had been amazing.

Zo-Zo leaned toward Robin. "I wish my grandmother had a cool boyfriend like him."

With a pleased smile on her face, Griff tucked Finn's letter into the pocket of her lavender fleece to read later.

Finished with the call, Gord walked back into the kitchen.

"Anything serious?"

"A bear broke in to someone's porch to get some blueberry pies. I'd better get out there before the man kills it." He waved and went out.

The phone rang again. The lines on Griff's face deepened.

"Will someone please throw that darn thing in the lake?"

Squirm mimicked picking up the phone and hurling it as far as he could. He burst out laughing. Then he noticed the stamp on one of the letters in the pile.

"Whoa! That's a Hercules beetle. I *love* those guys." He checked the postmark on the letter. "Hey! It's for us. From Costa Rica." He ripped the envelope open with his teeth and scanned through it.

"It's from some guy named Carlos. Says he's a conservationist down there. And that leatherback turtles are in big trouble."

Robin craned her head closer to Squirm. The first word on the page was written in big, black letters.

HELP!

Robin felt a thrum going all the way down her legs.

CHAPTER
FOUR

"What does it say?" Zo-Zo asked, craning her head toward the letter.

Knowing Squirm was a slow reader, Robin read it quickly. "The guy says he saw our website, thinks it's great, and wants us to go there and help him set up a turtle sanctuary. To save leatherbacks."

Zo-Zo's eyebrows did a quick high jump. "Wow. I'd *love* to go to Costa Rica."

Robin felt as if fireworks were shooting off in her chest. Going to Costa Rica would be amazing. But helping to set up a turtle sanctuary in Costa Rica would be *beyond* amazing.

"There's a link to the guy's website." Squirm reached for his tablet and typed in the link.

A page came up. All it had on it was a photograph of a turtle and a name: The Playa Tortuguitas Sanctuary.

"Not much of a website," Squirm said.

"I guess he's just getting started," Robin said. She sympathized with him. She knew what it was like to start an animal sanctuary from scratch. It wasn't easy.

"Look, there's other links further down," Zo-Zo said. "Click on the YouTube one."

Squirm did, and a huge turtle appeared on the screen, its flippers feathering through an ocean of blue-green water.

The turtle looked magical, Robin thought. As if it were flying through the water, not swimming.

"I love leatherbacks," Griff said softly.

Robin stared. The turtle was gigantic, prehistoric-looking, with large, unblinking eyes as big as tennis balls. Golden light shimmered on the tiles of its leathery shell.

The scene shifted. It was night now, and the leatherback was lumbering along the sand beach, its enormity even more apparent.

"Whoa. It's as big as I am," Squirm said.

Zo-Zo pushed her glasses closer to her eyes. "Bigger."

Griff leaned toward the screen. "Wouldn't be easy pushing a heavy body like that along a beach."

Squirm scrolled down and read some of the information that was on the bottom of the page. "Says here that they can weigh up to five hundred kilograms."

Griff scrunched up her face. "What's that in pounds? I can never do the math."

Zo-Zo laughed. "Over a thousand."

Squirm moved his cursor back to the video. "Look! She's making a nest!"

The turtle was now using her large, wing-like flippers to make what looked like a bed in the sand. Using her back flippers like shovels, she dug a deep chamber and began dropping her eggs into it.

"They're so big!" Robin cried.

Griff squeezed Robin's shoulders. "Goodness. Big as grapefruits."

Griff's voice was quiet, almost reverential. Robin felt quiet too. They were watching something special, very special.

Robin watched, mesmerized, as dozens and dozens of eggs were dropped into the sandy womb.

Suddenly, hands appeared and grabbed the eggs.

"Oh no!" Robin felt her stomach twist.

"Poachers," Griff spat.

The video showed someone pulling the eggs out of the hole in the sand and putting them into a large sack. Then the video showed a dark silhouette of a man walking away, a bulging bag at his side.

Robin tried to swallow, but she couldn't. How could someone steal babies? Babies! She wanted to run after the man and yank the bag away from him.

"Whoa," Squirm said. His face was contorted and grim. Even his freckles looked sullen and unhappy. He scrolled down the page again.

"Says here only one in a thousand turtles survives."

"That's egregious," Griff said.

Squirm looked up at Griff. "What's eg — egree —"

"Egregious? It means 'as bad as things can get.'"

Robin began to pace. A gang of feelings was running through her. Those odds were terrible. Worse than any other species she knew.

"How come so few survive?" Zo-Zo asked.

Griff wrung her huge hands together. "Poachers, for one thing. As the video showed, they dig up the eggs as soon as they're laid and sell them."

Hot, prickly indignation filled Robin's chest. Those eggs belonged to Mother Nature, not some stupid poacher.

Squirm looked confused. "They sell them? Why? Do they taste really good or something?"

Zo-Zo dug her elbow into him and clicked her tongue.

Squirm's freckles bunched together in confusion. "What?"

Griff tried to explain. "The poachers tell people the eggs will give them special powers. For sex. Or for healing illnesses. Which of course is a load of C-R-A-P. Same story with bear paws. Poachers tell people bear paws can heal all kinds of things. Which of course is just a bunch of baloney. It's just greed. Greed, greed, and more greed. Makes me ashamed to be part of the human race sometimes."

Robin nodded. She didn't want to be part of the human race either sometimes. "I think we should help Carlos."

Squirm's freckles looked as if they were going to pop right off his face. "But we're so far away!"

"I think we should go to Costa Rica! And help the leatherbacks," Robin said. A thrum of energy shot up her spine.

Zo-Zo jumped up and clapped her hands. "Yes!"

Robin grinned. As always, Zo-Zo was as eager to start an adventure as she was.

Griff threw her hands up. They flapped through the air like startled birds. "Let's go this afternoon. Nothing to do around here."

Robin looked at her grandmother. "Griff, they *need* us."

"So do the animals in this neck of the woods," Griff said. "It's spring. No time to even blow your nose."

Squirm did a drum roll on his thigh. "The insects are supposed to be *amazing* in Costa Rica. There's like thousands of species that we don't have in Canada." He pulled some jujubes from his pocket and began to juggle them.

"We should check out what a flight to Costa Rica costs," Zo-Zo said.

"Hold your horses, everyone," Griff said. "This is moving *way* too fast."

"I like fast," Zo-Zo said, spinning in place.

"I know, but not everyone works at the speed of light like you do," Griff said. "I don't, anyway." She reached for the shelter's log book and began to leaf through it.

"Last spring we rescued five baby raccoons, two bears, three squirrels, an owl, two hummingbirds, a heron, a beaver, and a porcupine. From the way the phone's ringing, there will be even *more* rescues to do this year. What about them? I don't want to burst any bubbles, but it seems to me we're full up helping our own animals."

Robin felt her nostrils flare. "But the leatherbacks are almost extinct, Griff. *Extinct!*" She blew the air out of her mouth with such ferocity that her lips flapped.

"Whoa, you guys, whoa," Squirm said, looking from his grandmother to Robin. "Carlos says right here that nesting season is in December, so if we go, it won't be until then anyway. When The Wild Place isn't even open."

Robin felt herself calm down. The thrumming in her body was only a slight humming now — the kind an engine makes when it's idle and waiting for the action to begin.

Keeping her voice even, she turned to her grandmother. "If we go to Costa Rica and help this guy set up a turtle shelter, we might have a chance at saving a whole *species*." If she could save a whole species, it would feel great. Beyond great.

Griff's blue eyes softened. "Let's take the first step, then. Write this Carlos fellow. Find out what he's got in mind."

"I'll email him," Robin said. Somehow, she had to get Griff interested in going. They would need an adult, and as far as Robin could figure, her grandmother was the only option. Zo-Zo's mom was living with that creep in another town so she wasn't a possibility, Zo-Zo's dad had the town newspaper to run, and Gord, her dad, had to be at The Wild Place to handle the medical side of things — so Griff would be the only one who could go.

The door opened and Robin's dad came in.

Squirm stopped juggling. "Guess what, Dad! We've been invited to Costa Rica to save turtles."

"Yeah?" Gord smiled. "What bank are you going to rob?"

Robin winced. *Right.* She'd forgotten about that. The Wild Place bank account was empty. It always was this time of year. But it would fill up over the summer as they rescued animals and people made donations.

"We'll have to do some fundraising, that's all," Robin said. It wasn't her favourite thing to do, but it had paid for their whale-saving adventure with Finn a while back.

"We could go during the winter holidays," Zo-Zo said. "Add on a few weeks. The teachers can give us work so we don't fall behind. Like they did when we went to the Antarctic."

"Yeah," Robin said. "We get two weeks, and if we add two more, we can go for like a month. A whole month!"

Zo-Zo threw her arms in the air. "That would be *so* cool!"

"Actually, it would be hot," Squirm said.

He and Zo-Zo burst out laughing.

Hot or cold, Robin knew one thing for certain. She was going to Costa Rica.

CHAPTER
FIVE

Over the next several weeks, Robin began emailing Carlos to find out more about him and the turtle sanctuary. The first exchanges were difficult because his English was poor and she wasn't exactly sure what he was trying to say. Was he having the same trouble understanding her? Probably.

Robin started to study Spanish. She found a translation site online, one that said Spanish words aloud. She listened to the words over and over again and tossed them into every conversation she could. Squirm got so fed up that he began covering his ears. Griff, who knew some Spanish, often helped her, and the two of them attempted some actual conversation.

"A passport might get you into a country," Griff said to Squirm, "but understanding the language is what will make the visit fun."

"Okay," Squirm said. "So what's the word for jujube in Spanish?"

Griff looked it up. "*Azufaifa.*"

"Cool," Squirm said, turning to Robin. "Can you ask Carlos if they have them down there?"

Robin nodded. "I think Carlos must be studying English just like I'm studying Spanish, because he's understanding more when I ask him stuff." She always reported what she found out to the others.

Email by email, she learned that the property Carlos was trying to make into a turtle sanctuary was an old abandoned building on a beach on the Pacific side of Costa Rica, in an area where leatherbacks were known to nest.

One day, when they were all eating a late breakfast, Robin pulled out a map and pointed to the exact area.

"That's where we're going," she said.

Ari made a face at her. "You wish."

Robin could smell the lemon in the tea Ari was drinking. "You'll see."

Squirm stared at the map. "Whoa. It looks like it's in the middle of nowhere."

"That might be good," Robin said. The more isolated they were, the fewer poachers there would be. She was nervous about poachers and trying not to think about them, but thoughts of them kept banging into her brain like flies at a closed window.

"Hey," Zo-Zo said, tapping the map. "You should put a map like this on the turtle sanctuary website."

"You're making the guy a website?" Ari asked.

Robin nodded. She felt good that Carlos had asked her to do this.

"You did a great job on The Wild Place website," Griff said. "You know how to do it."

She did. Carlos wanted his website in English as well as Spanish, so it was going to be a challenge to get it right.

"I still don't see why you have to go there," Gord said as he licked some maple syrup off his thumb. "You could do all the website work from here."

Robin groaned. "I *told* you, Dad. He wants help setting it up as well."

"And he wants us to help him collect turtle eggs," Zo-Zo added.

Robin looked at her dad. So far, he hadn't been very supportive of them going to Costa Rica, and she needed him to be. "Carlos wants every single turtle egg to survive. He spends hours patrolling the beach. And brings the eggs back to the hatchery he's built. Just to make sure they're safe."

Her father was listening, so she kept going.

"If we help him collect eggs, even for a few weeks, Carlos says that could make a big difference in the whole leatherback population."

Her father nodded, and Robin grinned at him. Was she starting to win him over?

"Goodness," Griff said, her eyes glinting. "Imagine coming back to Canada knowing you'd helped put hundreds of eggs in a safe place."

"It would be a bit like putting money in the bank," Gord said. "An environmental bank."

"Yeah," Squirm said. "We'd be like shovelling snow up here and baby turtles would be breaking out of their shells down there, running into the ocean."

They were all quiet for a moment, staring into the middle of the table as if it contained a screen showing dozens of baby turtles scuttling across the sand.

Robin pushed her foot against Squirm's leg under the

table and gave him a covert thumbs up. Sometimes her brother was the best.

Later, just before Robin went to bed, she pulled out her journal. She had to get a better sense of all that needed to be done. She wrote a list:

1. Learn Spanish
2. Arrange time away from school
3. Stop thinking about poachers
4. Raise money

The language thing she was already getting on top of. The school issue wasn't going to be a problem as long as her dad and Griff were on board, which she felt was starting to happen.

Her biggest problem was going to be number 3. She stared at the word *poachers*. Poachers scared her ever since she'd seen that video of them stealing turtle eggs.

When her mother was alive, she'd always told Robin to get more information whenever she started to feel anxious. Robin knew that's what she needed to do, so she picked up her phone and sent Carlos a text asking him directly if the sanctuary had poachers around.

A few minutes later, her phone pinged.

Poachers want eggs, not want bother tourists.

Robin frowned. He hadn't really answered her question, and she was thinking about what she could say next, when another text came in.

How is money raising?

Early on, Carlos had written that he'd take care of their food and accommodation if they could raise the money for the flights. Zo-Zo had researched the options, but the cost had made their jaws drop. It seemed so far beyond their means that Robin hadn't even begun to think of ways to raise it. But she didn't want to tell Carlos that, so she thumbed in only one word: *Slowly.*

Carlos texted an unhappy face, then said he was going out on patrol and left the conversation. Robin started a new journal page and began brainstorming ways to raise money.

- Make a flyer
- Have bake sales
- Rake leaves
- Babysit
- Do odd jobs

All the same things they had done to raise money for the Antarctic trip.

First thing the next morning, she began making a flyer. She put a large picture of a leatherback turtle on some neon-green paper and then wrote a description of the project underneath, with an appeal for donations. She put the flyer at the front of the shelter where anyone who came in would see it and placed an empty jar beside it.

When Griff saw it, she put a ten-dollar bill in the jar "to get things started."

That helped, and other people made donations too.

Over the next few weeks, she and Zo-Zo and Squirm did all the things on the list. Money trickled in. Meanwhile, her worries about poachers continued to eat away at the ripe peach of her enthusiasm like marauding ants.

When their fundraising efforts didn't bring in the dollars they needed, the likelihood of the trip actually happening started to erode. Summer ended and classes began, and Robin found herself getting caught up in all the usual school activities. Days went by without her writing Carlos, then weeks. What was the point of writing Carlos if they didn't have the money to go?

By the beginning of autumn, the idea of going to Costa Rica was barely alive. All her enthusiasm had disappeared. Like that acorn Griff had given her.

CHAPTER
SIX

The trees around The Wild Place began to sing with colour as the autumn blossomed into fullness. The Wild Place had released nearly all the hurt and abandoned animals they'd taken in during the spring and summer, and there were actually empty cages in the barn. Nonetheless, there were still calls coming in.

Just that morning, Robin and her father had been called out to help a young moose that had gotten its hooves caught between the slats of a picket fence. Moose were huge animals, and her father made her stay well behind him as she endeavoured to pass him tools to cut the slats away. She kept her movements slow and steady, but still, the moose twitched in distress. She made herself breathe and stay calm, knowing that the animal would take its cue more from her energy than from her actions.

She was relieved when her father pulled off the last picket and the moose bounded away, heading for the tranquil safety of the woods. It amazed her that an animal so big, so awkward, and so lumbering could move so fast.

Now Griff was taking another call. Robin tried to listen in as she hefted an armload of saplings for Barney, the beaver who was still recuperating from some nasty burns on his face and paws. A month or so ago, an irate cottager had dynamited his hut. He was doing well now, and Robin hoped they'd be able to release him in the next few weeks — far from the upset cottager.

Robin cocked her ear, trying to get a sense of the problem on the phone. She didn't want to have to deal with anything too involving. Today, Zo-Zo was visiting her mother in another town but hoped to be back by dinner, and the two of them had plans to make pizza at her place. Robin didn't want to do a rescue that would get in the way of that. She thought of getting Squirm to do her stint in the shelter this afternoon, but he was trying to get an assignment done for school. He'd read a draft of it to her yesterday. It was titled, "Why I Want to Be a Bug Doctor."

"Yes, Officer," Griff was saying. "I'm listening, but I'm not sure I have this right … a *goose* is *what*? Banging on your door?" She looked over at Robin, an amused smile spreading over her wide mouth.

At least it didn't sound life-threatening, Robin thought. To the man or the goose. She was glad. She wasn't in the mood for anything intense.

Griff got directions and grabbed her keys. "Just when you think you've heard it all …"

They climbed into the van and sped down the lane. Robin waited for her grandmother to share the details of the call. She didn't have to wait long.

"That was Officer Ryan," Griff said. "Nice guy. Big fan of our work."

"So what's the problem?" Robin asked, wanting Griff to get to the nugget of things.

"He's on patrol near the industrial park. By Smith's pond. Apparently there's a goose that won't stop pecking the side of his cruiser."

"Weird," Robin said.

Griff nodded. "Said he's shooed it away a few times, but it just comes back and starts pecking again. He doesn't want to hurt the goose but says if his cruiser gets dented, he's going to be in trouble. Big trouble."

Robin couldn't figure it out. "What do you think the goose wants?"

"Haven't a clue," Griff said, rubbing her lower jaw with one hand as she steered with the other. "But animals always have their reasons. That I know for sure."

Robin stared out the van window. The trees at the edge of the field were a fiery orange and red. They looked as if they'd been lit with a match.

"Do they have autumn in Costa Rica?" Griff asked.

Robin shrugged. How would she know?

"You should take some pictures of the trees with your phone today," Griff said. "Send them to Carlos. He'll be amazed." She was quiet for a moment. "I've been wanting to ask you for a while, how's the fundraising going?"

"It's pathetic."

Robin felt disappointed in herself. When she'd first thought about going to Costa Rica, the idea had been as bright and buoyant as a balloon, but it seemed to have lost its air now and had slunk from the ceiling to the floor. "I thought with all the time we had it would be easy to raise the money."

"Sometimes when you have a lot of time, it works against you," Griff said. "It takes the pressure off."

She turned off the main road. "Do you still think going to Costa Rica is the right thing to do?"

Robin glanced at her grandmother. "What do you mean, 'right'?"

Griff tilted her head one way and then the other. "Some things are just right to do. They fit us inside. Even if they don't always fit on the outside."

Robin closed her eyes for a moment. The feeling was clear: helping someone set up an animal shelter would be something she'd be proud of for the rest of her life. So maybe it *was* one of those right things.

"I think it would be awesome," she said to Griff.

"Something must be getting in the way, then. What's spooking you about the trip?"

Robin sighed. There was no point in trying to hide anything from Griff. "It's the poacher thing. It freaks me out."

"I thought Carlos said that most of the poachers were on the Caribbean side of Costa Rica?"

Robin nodded. "Yup. That's what he said." But it didn't matter. Her fear seemed to be huddled in the corner of a soundproof room, unable to hear.

Griff put on her turn signal. Its *tick, tick, ticking* filled the van. "Not surprising then that the fundraising has cooled off. Sounds like *you* have cooled off. If you're half-hearted, the fundraising is going to be half-hearted too."

She turned down a narrow lane. "I bet if you got totally clear and committed about going, the money would show up."

The police cruiser appeared ahead, parked on the side of the road near the industrial buildings a short distance from a pond. A large Canada goose was strutting nervously alongside it. Robin watched as the goose lurched toward the cruiser, thrust out its long black neck, and pecked the car's side.

Rat-tat-tat.

Griff parked several metres behind the cruiser. "Better give the girl a lot of room." She turned off the van. "She sure looks like she's got her knickers in a knot."

The goose, noticing their arrival, shuffled from webbed foot to webbed foot and regarded them warily. Then it banged its beak against the cruiser door again.

Rat-tat-tat.

"Ouch," Griff said. "No wonder Ryan is worried about his car getting dented. Goose beaks can pack a powerful punch. They can peck out an eye in a nanosecond."

Great, Robin thought, staring at the goose. *Just what I need. A furious goose.*

"What do you think it wants?"

"You'll have to ask the goose," Griff said, getting out of the van. "I'll go talk to the officer."

Robin watched as Griff made her way to the passenger side of the cruiser, staying as far away from the goose as she could.

Robin opened her door and eased herself out, trying not to alarm the goose.

Standing a safe distance from it, she whispered, "Be nice, goose. I'm not here to hurt you. I'm here to help."

The goose jerked its head in her direction, its black eyes sharp and alert. Impatiently, it shifted its feet, then turned and waddled toward the pond. Sensing that it wanted her to follow, Robin did. The goose raised its wings and fluffed them down again as if saying, "Finally."

Robin followed the goose through some tall reeds that surrounded the pond. The reeds were wet, and soon her jeans were soaked. She was just about to turn back when she saw a second goose. It was smaller and agitated and tried to move away when it saw Robin, but it couldn't. Something was immobilizing its legs. Robin craned forward and saw fishing line tangled around its feet.

Quickly, Robin went back to the van and spoke to her grandmother. Together they got a blanket out of the rescue bag and some oven mitts and scissors, then walked back to where the geese were.

Griff talked quietly to both birds, using a soft, slow tone that was calming even to Robin. All the while, she was moving slowly but surely toward the second goose, telling it what she and Robin were going to do. When she was close enough to the tangled-up goose, she swiftly but expertly lifted the blanket and draped it over the bird, covering its body and head.

"Be quick," she said to Robin as she held the goose firmly against her chest.

Robin stepped forward and cut the fishing line from the feet that were dangling from the opening in the bottom of the blanket. Two snips and she was done.

She moved back, and Griff did as well, tugging the blanket away as she did. The goose shook itself, as if making sure everything was still in its right place, and trundled off.

"You're welcome," Griff called after it.

The second goose followed, and Robin and Griff watched the birds ease themselves into the dark water of the pond. They swam off, carving a long arrow into the surface of the deep, green water.

Griff folded up the blanket. "Don't you just love the way geese take care of each other?"

They gathered up their things.

"No wonder she was pecking on the cruiser's door," Griff said. "She was asking for help. *Ha!*" She thumped her hand on Robin's back. "Good thing you were listening."

Robin smiled. Animals were smart, a lot smarter than most people gave them credit for.

"Courageous," Griff said. "Strutting up to the cruiser like that. Banging on the door. That must have been scary for her. Risky. But sometimes taking risks is the right thing to do."

Robin thought about Costa Rica and the poachers. "But what if the risk you want to take feels too big?"

Griff laughed. "Risks usually feel too big." She paused for a moment, then added, "You have to kind of creep your way up to risks. Baby step by baby step. Even though your legs are shaking." She put her arm around Robin's waist and gave her a slight squeeze. "Speaking of steps, we should get back to Officer Ryan. He's going to wonder what happened to us."

Robin fell in beside Griff as they walked through the reeds.

"So what would a baby step be in terms of going to Costa Rica?" Griff asked.

Robin knew the answer right away. "Setting a date to go."

"Sounds like a good start."

"And if we don't raise enough money?"

Griff stopped walking and looked at Robin. Her blue eyes matched the sky. "Oh, my sweet girl, you've got to stop focusing on your doubts. Every time you do that, you feed them. And they get bigger. Just focus on what you want. And act 'as if.' That's all you have to do. If you start acting like you're going to Costa Rica, getting a travel date, starting to organize what you'll need to take with you, all that stuff, things will start to happen to make the trip a reality. Believe me."

They were nearly back at the cruiser now.

"I'll tell Officer Ryan that he doesn't have to worry about his cruiser getting dented anymore."

Robin got into the van and waited. She stared at the big, puffy clouds. One of them looked like a turtle. After she'd watched that video about the leatherback and the egg poaching, she'd felt so fired up. The heat of that fire had burned up all her fear. But the fear had come back and just wouldn't go away. It was clear to her now that the fear wasn't *going* to go away. What she had to do was go forward anyway. Just like Griff said.

Griff got in the van.

"I've decided," Robin said.

"Decided what?"

"To go to Costa Rica."

An impish grin erupted on Griff's face, jumping from one part of her mouth to another. She handed Robin a folded piece of paper.

"Well, this will come in handy then. It's from Officer Ryan."

Robin opened the piece of paper. It was a cheque. For a large sum of money.

Griff turned the key and the van roared to life. "That should give a boost to your Costa Rica fund."

Robin grinned just as a goose honked way up in the sky.

CHAPTER SEVEN

"Let's go, let's go, let's go," Griff said as she strode to the car and stuffed her big blue suitcase in beside the others. "The airport's a long way, and we don't want to miss the plane."

Hurrying behind her grandmother, Robin shoved her backpack on top of the pile. The whale stickers from their previous trip were all peeling, and she tried to slap them down again, but her hands were sweaty. She felt jittery. Adventures like this were exciting, but nerve-wracking too. Did she have everything? Her phone? Passport? Sunblock?

She checked her watch. It was ten to six. And not even light out. She looked around. Where was Zo-Zo? If she didn't show up soon, they were going to be late.

Griff called back toward the house. "Come on, Squirm! Get a move on. We're running behind."

Robin climbed into the cold car and arranged herself amongst the bags. From the number of them, it looked like they were going away for a year, not a month. Worriedly, she felt for her fanny pack. It was still there, around her waist, just as it had been a few minutes ago.

She unzipped it and checked for the tenth time to see if it still held her passport and money. Remarkably, it did.

She took out a beige envelope and counted the crisp, green twenty-dollar bills. Her father had given them a substantial donation a few weeks ago, and this was the cash left over from buying the plane tickets.

"Your mother started a small education fund for you kids before she died," he had told both her and Squirm. "I think this trip is educational enough for it to qualify. I know she'd want to support it."

Robin felt goosebumps remembering. Her mother had made this trip possible. And now, this morning, it was as if her mother was with her somehow.

If only.

She ran her fingers over the smooth bills, then stuffed them back into the envelope and zipped it into the pack again. Even though her mother's little present was out of sight now, it felt good to know it was there. Like it was good to know there was sunshine above the clouds, even when you couldn't see it.

Relentless nosed her face into Robin's lap and put her paws on Robin's thighs.

"I know. I hate saying goodbye too," Robin said, looking into her dog's mournful eyes. She stroked her dog's silky black ears, then gently eased Relentless out of the car again. As she did, she cast her eyes to the upstairs window and saw Ari looking down at her.

Amazed that her sister had yanked herself from sleep to wave goodbye, Robin surprised herself and blew Ari a kiss. Ari blew one back. Robin felt her eyes watering and looked away. Why was she getting all sucky over leaving her sister? Because she was a wuss, that's why.

A forest-green Toyota pulled up and Zo-Zo got out, waving goodbye to her dad as casually as if she were going to the mall for the afternoon. Her coat was open and Robin could see her T-shirt. It had a neon-orange sun on the front and the words *Costa Rica*. She strode toward Robin.

"Cool shirt, eh? My dad gave it to me as a going-away present."

"I need sunglasses just to look at you," Griff said, getting in.

Zo-Zo settled beside Robin in the back seat. Suddenly, she grabbed her backpack. "Sunglasses! My prescription sunglasses!" Quickly, she tapped the pocket of her backpack. "Good, I've got them." She touched the oversized glasses on her face as if to make sure they were there too.

Robin stared at Zo-Zo's huge glasses. She'd hate to have something that big on her face all the time.

"You know me," Zo-Zo said. "I'm blind as a bat without my glasses."

Gord got into the driver's seat and Griff shouted out the window. "Squirm. We're leaving!"

Squirm came blasting out of the house, a book shoved under his arm.

"Wow, Squirm's got ears," Zo-Zo said.

"He got a haircut," Robin said. Now, not only did his ears stick out more, but his freckles looked browner and bolder than ever.

Griff moved closer to Gord to make room for Squirm, and Gord started the car.

Griff looked over her shoulder at the house.

"Think Ari will be all right?"

"Mom, she's fifteen," Gord replied, putting the car in reverse. "I'll drop you off and be back by midafternoon."

"Goodbye, house," Squirm crooned. "Goodbye, dog, goodbye, ant farm. Goodbye, insect collection." As the car sped down the laneway, he opened his insect identification book and began to look through the pictures.

Zo-Zo checked her watch. "By this time tomorrow, we'll be on a beach, soaking up that hot, hot sun."

Squirm leaned over the seat. "I showed you guys the Hercules beetle, right?"

Robin nodded. *Like a hundred times.*

He held up a book and pointed to a picture. "That's it there. It's like ginormous."

Robin cringed. It was bigger than her hand.

Squirm's eyes widened. "It can carry 850 times its body weight."

"That's like you lifting a whale," Gord called from the front.

"Good thing it's not poisonous," Squirm said. "But a ton of insects down there are."

Zo-Zo eyebrows shot up into her forehead. "In Costa Rica?"

"Yup," Squirm said.

Robin grimaced. She didn't want to hear that. Not right now.

"Scorpions, for one thing. 'Specially the baby ones."

"Why the baby ones?" she asked.

"They shoot all their venom instead of holding some back, like adults do," he said.

She wished she hadn't asked.

Squirm flipped to another page. "Check this out."

Robin stared at the picture of the scorpion. At least that's what she thought it was. It had what looked like lobster claws in front, but at the back, curled in the air, ready to strike, was a menacing stinger.

Great, she thought. Just great.

"Everyone will have to remember to shake out their shoes before putting them on," Gord said.

Squirm flipped through more pages of his insect book, clearly enthralled with all the options in Costa Rica. "There's scarabs, cockroaches, snakes —"

Robin let out a loud moan. "*Squirm!*"

She didn't mind bugs. She'd grown up with them. But waving away a few mosquitoes or black flies was one thing — dealing with poisonous insects was another.

"Remember Mom and snakes?" Squirm asked.

Shut up, Squirm. Shut up!

"She had a real thing about snakes, didn't she?" Gord said. "She was never afraid of them. I remember how impressed I was by that when I met her. In fact, she *liked* snakes, had a kind of kinship with them. She —"

The car, her father, and everything else faded and became distant as Robin went back in her memory. She was eight and her mother hadn't gotten sick yet. The two of them were walking in the woods when her mother pointed at something hidden among some leaves and sticks.

It was a snake. But the snake was doing something incredible. It was pulling itself right out of its skin.

She and her mother had watched, enthralled.

When the snake was done, it slithered away, leaving a long rope of translucent skin behind.

Her mother had picked it up and given it to her, laying it in Robin's hands as if it were a silver necklace.

"There you go, my little bird."

My little bird.

It was something her mother sometimes called her. It made Robin's eyes sting to remember.

Zo-Zo spoke, bringing her back to the present moment. "I wish I'd met your mom," she said. "She sounds so cool."

Robin swallowed hard.

There was a long, quiet moment, then Griff slid a CD into the car's audio system. A man's deep voice filled the air with Spanish.

"*Gracias. Muchas gracias.*"

Squirm groaned.

"*Soy canadiense.*"

Squirm turned it down and looked up at Griff. "What's the word for scorpion?"

"*El escorpión*," she said. "But let's talk about something other than spiders and insects."

Squirm shut the bug book and picked up another. "Okay, then let's talk about turtles!" He pointed to another earmarked page. "Bet you guys didn't know that sea turtles can drown —"

Robin sighed. Was there no way to shut him up? He was acting like an out-of-control windup toy. She wished now that she'd brought along a bag of jujubes so she could stuff his mouth with them.

She stared outside. The fields looked brittle and brown. Usually by now there was snow, lots of it. It was weird that there wasn't any. And that it was so warm.

Squirm poked her. "Did you know that, Robin?"

She rolled her eyes. "Know what?"

"That turtles have lungs, like we do. They can stay underwater for a long time, but they still have to come up for air. If they don't, like if they get caught underwater in a net or something, they drown."

"Is that why they're so endangered?" Zo-Zo asked. "I mean, if each turtle lays dozens of eggs, and they do that a couple of times a year, you'd think there'd be millions of them."

"There used to be," Griff said in a sad, low voice.

"Yeah," Gord said, "but more and more of their habitat is being destroyed all the time. And then there's poaching."

Poaching. There was that word again. Robin felt her muscles tighten.

Squirm's nose was back in his book. "Wow," he said. "Says here that sea turtles, like leatherbacks, can't pull their heads into their bodies like land turtles can. I didn't know that."

Robin gave Zo-Zo a *when the heck is he going to shut up* look.

Zo-Zo unzipped her pack and pulled out some neon-orange flip-flops. She took off her shoes and socks and put them on.

"I want to get into the mood."

She pulled out a plastic bottle of suntan lotion and began smearing the creamy white lotion on her arms. The smell of coconut filled the air.

Griff turned in her seat and smiled. "Aren't you jumping the gun a little?"

Zo-Zo grinned. "You know me — I like jumping the gun."

Squirm made a pistol out of his fingers and fired it at her. "Pow! Pow!"

Ignoring him, Zo-Zo peered into a pocket of her suitcase. "I've got SPF 30, 40, even 50. I figure we're going to need it. It's supposed to be sunny down there all day, every day. And hot. Hot and steamy. Just how I like it."

Robin flinched. Hot and steamy? Like the air in a bathroom after a shower? She wasn't good in wet heat. Never had been. Suddenly, she felt full of anxiety.

Beside her, Zo-Zo was organizing things in her pack. She seemed so nonchalant, as if she were getting ready for school, not getting on a plane to go to a foreign country. Robin wished she could be as relaxed. All this stuff Griff said about her courage was just a bunch of bunk. Nice words to make her feel better.

Zo-Zo put her earbuds in and faint reggae music escaped from them.

Feeling forlorn, Robin looked out the window. Something caught her eye. A large black animal was running in the field alongside the road. But something was wrong — it kept tripping and bumping into trees and shrubs. As if it couldn't see where it was going. Was it blind?

Her father rubbernecked his head around to look at it too and slowed the car.

Griff checked her watch. "We don't have a minute to spare."

"It's a bear!" Robin cried. But what did it have its head stuck in? Some sort of bucket?

The bear bashed into a rock, fell, then scrambled up again.

Gord pulled the car over to the side of the road.

"We can't stop!" Squirm almost shouted. "We're already behind."

Gord leaned forward and turned to his mother. "What's that on its head? A honey bucket?"

Robin tracked the bear as it zigzagged around the field. It must have poked its head in some farmer's honey bucket to have a good lick and gotten stuck. No wonder it was acting crazy.

Zo-Zo gripped the back of the front seat. "We should get going."

"Yeah," Squirm said.

The bear bumbled toward the road. A pickup truck appeared around the curve and barrelled toward it.

Robin covered her face.

The driver blasted his horn. The sound of it went on and on.

She held her breath. The truck thudded into the bear — in her mind. But when she opened her eyes, the bear had somehow shot back into the field.

Zo-Zo grabbed Robin's arm. "Don't even think about it."

Robin yanked herself free and bolted out of the car. She had to help. Even if it was just to shout at the bear until it ran back into the woods. She began running toward it.

"Come back!" Squirm yelled behind her.

"We'll miss the plane," Zo-Zo hollered.

Robin didn't hear them. She was shouting too loudly herself, shouting at the bear, waving her arms wildly as she tried to chase it to safety. Although why she was using her arms, she didn't know. The bear would not be able to see her.

Suddenly, the air was split by the crack of a gun.

In front of her, the bear staggered, then slowly fell to the ground, slumping in a heap.

Her father came up behind her, rifle in hand.

As Robin approached the bear, her heart hammered. Its fur was coal black, thick and glossy. The claws at the ends of its arms and legs were long and razor sharp. It wasn't a big bear, but it was muscular and beautiful and exuded a smell of ancient, primitive things.

Robin wiped her sweaty palms on her jeans as she watched her father pull the anaesthetic dart out of the bear's side.

"Good shot, Dad," she said.

He nodded toward the bucket. "Why don't you be the hero here?"

Her legs felt shaky, but she spread them wide and put one hand on either side of the plastic tub. Leaning back, she pulled for all she was worth. Within seconds there was a deep-sounding *thunk* like a cork coming out of a bottle. The bucket popped off the bear's head so quickly, she fell back and away. Her father helped her up. She whacked the skiff of snow off her jeans.

"Way to go," her dad said. He handed her the honey bucket. The bear's claws had cut deep grooves into its plastic sides.

"Let's keep it as a souvenir," he said. "No one will believe us otherwise."

Robin grinned at him as they moved quickly back to the car.

Griff, Squirm, and Zo-Zo all stared at her as she got back in. Robin settled into her seat. All her anxiety had gone now. She felt strong and alive. Ready to get on the plane. She closed her eyes. There was nothing like a rescue to get her in the mood for an adventure.

Okay, Costa Rica. Here I come!

CHAPTER EIGHT

They made it to the airport with only minutes to spare and boarded the plane. Robin wedged herself between Griff and Zo-Zo and squeezed their hands hard as they taxied down the runway. When the plane rocketed up into the air, the speed and force of it took Robin's breath away.

The moment they reached their travelling altitude, the flight attendant brought around drinks and snacks. After that, there was a film. Robin started to watch it, but she was so tired, she fell asleep. She dreamed about a bear wandering freely in the woods. The next thing she knew, Griff was nudging her to fasten her seat belt as they were starting their descent into San José, Costa Rica.

When the plane touched down, Robin and Zo-Zo grinned at each other and slapped their open palms together in a high-five. Once they were off the plane, they headed immediately for the baggage area.

Zo-Zo pulled her backpack off the carousel and Griff helped Squirm with his.

"Geez, Squirm. What's in here? Rocks?"

"Books." Squirm grunted as he hefted his bag onto a cart. "I want to be able to identify every bug I see. In English."

Griff wrestled her own bag off the carousel and stood beside Robin while she waited for hers. It did not appear.

When there was no more luggage coming through the shoot, Griff dug out their baggage tags and headed over to an airline attendant, who spent several minutes trying to locate the bag.

"I've found it," the attendant finally said. "Unfortunately, it's still in Toronto. It never made it to the plane. Were you late checking in?"

Squirm groaned. He opened his mouth to say more, but Griff's fierce look stopped him.

"Detour, Squirm, detour."

"Detour" was Griff's code word for getting someone to take their talk in a new direction. Squirm closed his mouth.

The flight attendant told them they'd be notified when Robin's bag arrived and turned to another customer.

Robin sighed and walked away. It wasn't going to be fun not having her own clothes for a while, but she didn't regret stopping to help the bear. It had been the right thing to do.

"You can wear my stuff," Zo-Zo said easily.

They moved to the main part of the airport and looked around for Carlos. He'd sent one or two grainy photographs over the internet, but none of them knew exactly what he looked like.

"Maybe he's waiting outside." Griff steered the over-loaded cart through some glass doors, which made a swishing sound as they parted.

Robin stepped out of the airport building. Suddenly, it was as if someone had thrown a pail of steaming hot water at her. Perspiration sprang from every pore of her skin. She felt like she was in a sauna.

Zo-Zo threw her arms out to her sides in rapture. "It's just like I hoped. Hot, hot, hot!" She twirled on the spot.

Robin went back into the cool airport, parked herself in a chair where she could still see them, and waited. People bustled around her. Most of them had black hair and some shade of brown skin. Few were tall, but there were white people too, and people who looked Chinese or Asian. It was intriguing to see such a variety of ethnic backgrounds and to hear so many foreign languages. It was very different from what she saw and heard back home.

This is the big, wide world, she thought. She felt a bit uneasy about it; it was all so new and different, but it was also exciting.

After what seemed like a very long time, a rusty van pulled up outside. It had a turtle painted on its door. A bony arm reached through the open window and released a makeshift wire that was holding the door shut. A young man got out. Carlos. He was wearing cut-off shorts and a black, sleeveless shirt. Robin stared at him. Twig-thin, he looked as if his body might snap in two if it were bent in the wrong way. His eyes looked heavy, as if they carried the weight of the world.

He scanned the crowd as he forked his skinny fingers through his thick, wavy black hair and straightened as Griff came toward him.

"*Hola!*" he said warmly. "*Bienvenidos!*"

"*Gracias!*" Griff said back.

He shouted the same words to Squirm and Zo-Zo and began to shake everyone's hands. When Robin came out of the building, he shook hers too, his grip firm and determined. She smiled, noticing a line of small tattooed turtles running down his arm from his shoulder to his hand. There was a turtle tattoo on his palm as well, so when he took Robin's hand, it was like the turtle was being pressed right into her. When she pulled her hand away, it was thrumming. She hadn't felt that thrumming in a while.

Done with the introductions, Carlos turned and hefted their bags easily from the trolley into the van, and they headed off.

"Cool-looking guy," Zo-Zo whispered. Robin nodded.

They drove off with the windows rolled down. As they picked up speed, a lovely breeze streamed through the windows, and Robin flapped the cloth of her T-shirt so the air could move along her skin. As nice as that felt, it was too warm to cool her. Was it going to be this hot in Costa Rica all the time? She'd only been out in the open air for a short while but already felt as wet and slippery as a seal.

They drove away from the airport, and Robin could see a haze of tall buildings in the distance. That must be the city, she thought. Were they going to go there? She hoped not. It would be even hotter. To her relief, Carlos steered the van the other way, and they headed out into the countryside.

"Two-hour drive now," Carlos said. "Benita, my cousin, she making feast. She has son, Marcos. Same age Squirm. Diego, husband, he there too. He guards eggs."

"*Bueno*," Griff said. She smiled at Squirm. "You'll have someone to play with."

"Hope he likes bugs," Squirm said.

As they drove, there were fewer and fewer houses and buildings. Carlos waved his free hand toward the woods along the side of the road. It looked lush and beautiful. Hard to believe, Robin thought, that back in Canada it might be snowing.

"Everything still green," Carlos said. "Rainy season now. Just ending. Soon, all will turn brown. Then dry season."

Carlos continued to talk more about the variations in the weather in Costa Rica, but between the softness of his voice and the loudness of the wind, Robin could barely hear, so she finally sat back and just took in the scenery. Everything was deep rich green and moist looking.

As they drove, they passed some small villages, the houses jammed in close to each other. At one village Carlos pulled the van over to the side of the road, and kids in bright clothing appeared out of nowhere. One of them, a boy who looked not much older than Squirm, had a huge machete stuffed into his rope belt.

Carlos nodded to him, and the boy scampered up a palm tree. Robin looked up and saw bunches of coconuts at the top. The boy cut a bunch and tossed them to Carlos. He monkeyed back down, cut the tops off the coconuts, shoved paper straws into the openings, and gave one to each of them.

Squirm took a sniff. "Hey, this smells like suntan lotion."

Everyone laughed and piled into the van with their coconut drinks. Although Robin wished the drink was cooler, it tasted great.

"And completely recyclable," she said, nodding to the husk.

"Hey, yeah," Squirm said, laughing.

It was late afternoon by the time they turned into a narrow lane. There was a small sign at the beginning of it that read, El Refugio de la Playa Tortuguitas.

Squirm attempted to read it out loud. "What does playa tortu — tortug —"

"Beach of hatchlings," Carlos said as he manoeuvred the van up the bumpy lane.

"Finally, we're *here*!" Zo-Zo said.

Robin was jostled against the others as the van went up the lane, finally stopping in front of a dirty grey building. There were shingles missing from the roof, and one window had a piece of cardboard taped over it.

"Whoa," Squirm whispered.

Robin's eyes widened. The place was going to need a lot of work.

Carlos got out of the van.

"Remember, we're here for the turtles, not the aesthetics," Griff whispered to the kids as she grabbed her purse.

Not having a bag, Robin headed toward the building. She stopped walking. She could hear a man shouting. Then a woman shouting back.

Squirm came up beside her, then Zo-Zo and the three of them stood in a huddle of apprehension. Griff reached her arms around them protectively.

"Wait," Carlos said and rushed forward, disappearing into the building.

Carlos's voice could be heard now above the other man's, loud and reprimanding. Robin couldn't make out the words, he was talking so fast, but it sounded like he was trying to shut the other man up.

She turned to Griff, who knew more Spanish than she did. "What are they fighting about?"

Griff kept her voice low. "Something about foreigners."

Zo-Zo took a sharp breath. "He's calling us *foreigners*?"

"He says he doesn't want us here," Griff said.

Robin felt something tighten in her gut. "But we're here to help."

"Intense," Zo-Zo whispered.

A few minutes later, the shouting ended and Carlos appeared. He looked rattled and smiled awkwardly as he ushered them inside the building.

They entered a large room full of wooden tables that had benches on either side. A bulky, unshaven man wearing a multicoloured knitted hat was hunched over where he sat on one of the benches, looking down. He exuded the smell of cigarettes, an aroma Robin detested.

Robin thought at first that the man was looking down because he felt bad. She certainly would have felt bad if she'd been caught shouting by arriving strangers. But she saw that there was no remorse on the man's face — only sullen resentment. He didn't acknowledge them in any way.

Worried the man was going to feel her staring at him, Robin looked away.

Across from him in a little kitchen area was a plump young woman with a radiant face and round, sculpted cheekbones. She was doing her best to smile and had one arm around a young boy who looked about the same age as Squirm.

Carlos introduced them. He waved to the woman first.

"Benita. My cousin. *Ella es una gran cocinera*. Great cook." He pointed to the boy. "This is son, Marcos." The boy grinned as he leaned back against his mom.

They all looked at the man who'd been shouting. He still had not raised his head.

Carlos cleared his throat and motioned toward the sullen man. "Diego. Benita's husband. He guards hatchery."

Zo-Zo nudged Robin with her elbow then drew her index finger pointedly along her neck.

Robin followed Zo-Zo's gaze. Just under the collar of Diego's work shirt was a long pucker of skin, deathly white, running from his ear to his shoulder. What would make a scar like that? A cut from a knife? She shivered.

Robin and the others all said their names. Benita smiled as each of them spoke, as did Marcos. Diego stood up, scowled, and left the room.

"I don't think he likes us," Squirm said softly.

Marcos reached under his bench and picked up a small iguana.

"Pedro," he said proudly as two large dimples appeared on his moon-round face.

Squirm's face lit up. "Can I hold him? Please! I'll be careful, I'll —"

Tenderly, Marcos placed the iguana in Squirm's eager hands.

"Oh, the resilience of youth," Griff said and turned to Robin. "Let's get the rest of our stuff in."

Carlos helped them lug in their bags, taking them to a room beside the dining area that had four single beds along one wall. Robin claimed the bed beside the window. She was hoping she'd get more of a breeze there, and besides, it looked over a fenced-in area that she thought must be the egg hatchery.

No sooner had everyone unpacked than Carlos announced a walk in the forest. "Quick," he said. "Before eat."

Carlos led them down the road to a path that went into a dense thicket of trees. Robin expected it to be cooler there, as it always was in the woods in Canada, but it was just as hot and moist. But everything was lush and green and incredibly beautiful. Yellow, orange, and blue butterflies fluttered through the air.

Carlos talked quickly and animatedly, and Griff did her best to translate.

"Carlos says that in the dry season, all the flowers come out and there will be pink, white, and red orchids everywhere."

They walked on, and Robin could hear monkeys shrieking, parrots cawing, and birds singing.

"It's like *noisy* in here," Zo-Zo said, and they both laughed. But Robin was fascinated. Never before had she been in a forest so loud with life.

"Whoa!" Squirm said over and over again as Carlos pointed to different insects.

On their way back, when Carlos and the two boys were ahead, Robin turned to Griff.

"So what did that guy mean about foreigners? I don't understand."

Griff frowned. "People in developing countries sometimes get worried about their ways being taken over. They sometimes distrust outsiders."

Robin frowned. "But Carlos *asked* us to come."

"I know," Griff said. "But I'm guessing he overruled Diego to do that. And now we're dealing with the consequences."

Robin was thoughtful for a moment. "Maybe he'll come around when he sees how much help we can be."

"The place sure needs work," Zo-Zo said.

"And work we will," Griff said. "First thing tomorrow, let's have a meeting. Find out where Carlos wants us to start."

"Good idea," Robin said. There was a lot they could do. But it was Carlos's decision.

When they got back, they changed into bathing suits and ran along a sand path to the ocean. Robin threw herself in the water, expecting it to cool her off, but it was warm. And salty. But she could easily float in it. She liked that.

Benita called them for dinner. Hungry now, they went in to the dining area, still in their bathing suits and bare feet. Benita served up big platters of beans and rice wrapped in tortillas, and they ate quickly.

As Zo-Zo reached for seconds, she called over to Carlos. "After dinner, will you show us the hatchery?"

He nodded. As soon as they were finished eating, he led them to an area behind the building. As Robin had guessed, it was the same spot she'd seen from her bed in the dorm.

Smelling smoke, she spun around and saw Diego sitting in a deck chair at the far end of the hatchery. He was watching them.

She turned away, bumping into Zo-Zo, who was sidling up to her.

"That guy gives me the creeps," Zo-Zo said softly.

Robin nodded. He gave her more than the creeps. He frightened her. There was something mean about the man. Not wanting to think about him, she made herself focus on the turtle nests. Each one had a little stick marking its date of arrival and number of eggs.

"How long does it take for eggs to hatch?" Squirm asked.

Carlos held up six fingers.

"About sixty days," Robin said, remembering from all the reading she'd done.

Carlos nodded and continued. "I walk beach, find eggs, bring here. Diego guards. When hatch, I take back to beach."

"Can we walk the beach with you tonight?" Robin asked. She was eager to get out there, eager to see what they'd come to see: nesting leatherbacks.

"Yeah, can we?" Zo-Zo said. "Leatherbacks only drop their eggs at night, right?"

"Three hours before big tide," Carlos said. "Three hours after." He checked his watch. "Time get ready."

They all went into the dorm to get changed.

"Maybe we'll see our first leatherback," Robin said. Beside her, Zo-Zo was moving quickly, obviously as eager as she was to get out in search of nests.

Robin pulled her sneakers out from under the bed. She shoved her right foot into her running shoe.

"*Yeow!*"

Pain — excruciating pain — shot up from her big toe. She yanked her foot out of the shoe and shook her whole leg, violently trying to shake off whatever was biting her. When she did, she saw it scuttle across the floor.

A scorpion.

CHAPTER NINE

"*Owwwww!*"

Her toe was screaming with pain. She stood up and began hopping around the room on her good foot.

"*It hurts. It hurts. It hurts!*"

Zo-Zo ran over to her. "What happened? What —"

Robin pointed to the scorpion just as it scuttled into a crack in the wall and disappeared. "It bit me!"

Zo-Zo's eyes widened. "What bit you?"

It frightened Robin to even say the word, but she spat it out. "A scorpion!"

"A scorpion! Oh, *no!*"

"A scorpion?" Squirm raced into the room. "How do you know it was a scorpion? What did it look like?"

"Like, like that p-picture!" She kept hopping, but it didn't help. "The one you showed me." She'd never felt pain like this in her life. "P-pincers, curved tail …"

The blood drained from Squirm's face. "Griff! *Griff!*"

Griff lurched into the room. "What's the matter?"

Squirm's face was as grey as a tombstone. "A scorpion stung Robin."

Griff's hand flew to her chest. "Oh, my goodness!" She gently led Robin over to the closest bed and made her sit down. "You better stay still. Stay calm."

Stay still? Stay calm? How was that possible?

"The more agitated you are, the faster the venom will move through you," Griff said.

Squirm nodded. "Like a snakebite."

Griff turned toward the door. "Carlos! *Carlos!*"

"I'll find him," Zo-Zo said, and rushed off.

"My whole foot feels numb," Robin said. The venom was moving through her. What would happen when it reached her heart? Or her brain? Would she die?

Breathless, Zo-Zo sprinted back into the room, Carlos behind her. Marcos and Benita ran in as well.

Griff pointed to Robin's toe. "*El escorpión.*"

Carlos peered at Robin's red and swollen toe and shrugged. "Big hurt," he said. "I know." He pointed to a spot near his elbow between his turtle tattoos. "Stung here." Then he pointed to his right knee. "And here." He shrugged again. "Happens."

Zo-Zo's face filled with admiration. "Wow. You're tough. You act like a scorpion sting is no more than a mosquito bite."

"Should we take her to the doctor?" Griff asked.

Carlos turned to Robin and moved his thumb and forefinger close together, then apart. "Big? Little?"

Robin positioned her fingers a small distance apart. "Little."

Carlos's eyebrows shot up like the top half of two question marks. Squirm looked stricken.

A cold dread moved through Robin's chest. "What?

Tell me!"

"I think you got bitten by a *baby* scorpion," Squirm said. "Like I said, they're the worst."

Robin moaned. *Great.* Agitated, she wanted to stand up and start hopping around the room again but wouldn't let herself. She gritted her teeth and counted to ten, then counted to ten again. Anything to take her mind off the pain.

Carlos looked at Griff. "Big hurt, big swelling, then better. Doctor not needed. Unless worse."

Squirm got his laptop and began tapping into it. He read from the screen. "*Out of fifteen thousand scorpion species, only fifty are known to be deadly —*"

"Deadly!" Hot tears sprang to Robin's eyes. She didn't want to cry, not now, not in front of everyone.

Benita made the sign of the cross, and Marcos pushed his face into his mother's shoulder.

"Stop it, everyone!" Griff said. "We're scaring her!"

Robin could feel the numbness moving up her thigh.

"Wait," Squirm cried. "They're talking about scorpions out there in the world. *Not* the ones here." His eyes hurried down the page and he read again. "*None of the twelve species of scorpions found in Costa Rica are deadly.*" He looked up. "Phew!"

Zo-Zo pushed her thick glasses closer to her eyes and read aloud over Squirm's shoulder. "*Scorpion stings are mildly painful and involve numbness, tingling, and swelling.*"

Mildly painful? "Whoever wrote that has never been stung by one," Robin said.

Squirm looked serious again. "*Symptoms can include muscle twitching, drooling, sweating, and vomiting.*"

Robin grimaced. As horrible as these sounded, at least she wasn't going to die.

Griff turned to Carlos. "Is there a doctor nearby if we need one?"

Carlos nodded. "City."

"Hours away." Griff checked her watch.

Zo-Zo gently punched Robin's shoulder. "Sounds like it's going to hurt for a bit, then be fine. No big deal."

No big deal? Robin winced as if she'd just been stung a second time.

Zo-Zo tried to explain. "A big deal, but not a big deal, if you know what I mean."

Robin looked down. She was probably just being a wuss.

"I'll give you something for the pain." Griff went over to her suitcase and pulled out a bottle of pills. She gave Robin two along with a glass of water. "We'll see how you are in an hour or so." She took one of the sheets from the bed and draped it over Robin, careful not to graze the swollen toe.

"Better in morning," Carlos said, turning away. He walked over to the window and stared off into the black night. "Time for beach patrol."

Zo-Zo shook her head as if coming out of a trance. "Right."

Carlos waved to Zo-Zo. "Come."

Zo-Zo gave Robin an agonized look then turned back to Carlos.

"I couldn't. Robin is — I mean, she's in pain and I —"

Robin sighed. She could tell Zo-Zo wanted to go.

Carlos jerked his head toward Robin. "She be fine."

Zo-Zo hesitated. "I know, but —" Her eyes came back to Robin. "You won't feel a thing once those pills start working —"

Robin said nothing, but anger roiled through her stomach. How could Zo-Zo think of going off and leaving her behind?

Carlos waved to Zo-Zo again.

"Just an hour," Zo-Zo said to Robin. "I promise."

The two of them ran off and Squirm bolted after them, disappearing into the darkness before Griff could say a word to stop him.

Sighing, Griff eased herself in behind Robin on the bed so that her granddaughter's body leaned against her own.

"Oh, my sweet girl. Sometimes life is just so darned hard, it's all a person can do to stand it."

Robin could feel Griff's heart beating slowly and rhythmically. She found it soothing.

"I want to go home," she said simply.

Even saying the word "home" made her yearn to be there, yearn to be in her own bed, snuggling Relentless.

Griff took a moment before responding. "It's been a tough day, Robin. You're tired right now. And in pain. That's going to colour how you see things."

Robin yawned. She could feel the pills starting to muzzle the pain into submission. With Griff's arms holding her close, she felt safe and protected. She closed her eyes and let sleep, sweet sleep, gather her up and take her away from a world that she was only too glad to leave.

CHAPTER
TEN

When Robin woke up the next day, the other beds in
the room were empty. Where was everyone? She heard
Squirm laughing in the next room and the sound of
plates clattering. They must be having breakfast.

She sat up and checked her watch. She'd slept in.
Peering over the side of the bed, she scanned the floor
for bugs and reptiles, then swung her legs and feet out
of the bed. The T-shirt Griff had given her to sleep in
felt damp, but her foot felt better. Until she attempted to
stand. Then pain shot up her leg, and she sat down again.

"Hey, you're awake," Zo-Zo said, coming in with a
mug of papaya juice. "This is for you."

Robin made no move to take it. She didn't want
Zo-Zo thinking she could make up for going off last
night by just bringing her some juice.

Zo-Zo set the mug on the rickety table beside the
bed. "How're you feeling?"

Reluctantly, Robin pulled her foot back out from
under the sheet. The swelling had gone down, and her
toe was now pink rather than red.

"Does it still hurt?"

"Only when I try to stand," Robin said.

Zo-Zo looked at her with big, apologetic eyes. "Sorry I went off last night. It was stupid. I was just excited about seeing a leatherback. But we didn't see one. We didn't see anything. Just more and more beach."

Robin felt her resentment ease. At least she hadn't missed much.

Griff came in with a bowl of food and set it down so she could examine Robin's foot.

"Good thing we're not down here for a soccer tournament," she said when she was done. She handed Robin the bowl. Robin peered down at it. *Fried bananas?*

"Plantains," Griff said. "They're like bananas."

Robin squiggled up her nose and sniffed it. It smelled good, so she tasted it. It was delicious.

Griff went back to the kitchen.

There was an impish light in Zo-Zo's eyes. "I got the inside scoop on what's going on around here."

Robin sat up.

"Benita is Carlos's cousin. When Diego got fired from his old job for drinking, she begged Carlos to hire him to guard the hatchery. Carlos agreed, but only under the condition that Diego doesn't drink."

Robin shook her head. Her brain still felt fuzzy from sleep.

"But we were right," Zo-Zo said. "Diego doesn't want us here. Says we're foreigners. That's why he was shouting at Benita. He didn't want her cooking for us."

Robin felt a chill go up her back, even though she was hot.

Griff appeared in the doorway. "Carlos and I want to have a meeting. Just so we don't go running off in all directions like a bunch of chickens with their heads cut off. Come on into the dining room."

Robin lowered her voice. "Will Diego be there?"

"Don't know," Griff said. "But if he is, we're going to have to make the best of it. He's part of this place."

Robin told Griff what Zo-Zo had told her.

"Sounds like Diego might have a drinking problem." Griff frowned. "Poor man. If he does, that's just going to make everything worse." She shook her head. "But meanwhile, we still have a job to do, so let's get on with it. Zo-Zo, will you lend Robin something to wear?" Zo-Zo nodded and Griff went out.

Zo-Zo pulled out some brightly coloured shorts and tops for Robin to borrow, and in a few minutes, Robin, wearing a pair of crimson shorts and a sun-yellow shirt, was hobbling into the dining area with Zo-Zo at her side.

Squirm and Marcos were hunched over an insect book, laughing and pointing at pictures as they flipped through pages. Benita was washing up the breakfast dishes. Diego, who had been sitting with Carlos, scowled and sauntered out of the room.

A few minutes later, they were all seated around the same table and Griff turned to Carlos. "Now that you have some volunteers, what do you want us to do? We can collect eggs, we can do some painting and fixing, we could work on your website."

"Robin makes killer websites," Squirm said.

Carlos looked embarrassed. "Mine just beginning. Me just learning English and —"

89

Zo-Zo cut in. "No worries. We can help you say what you want to say."

"Since you already have something online, it won't take long to add to it," Robin said. "With my sore foot, there's not much else I can do anyway."

"Website important?" Carlos asked.

"If you want volunteers, it is," Griff said as she sipped some lemon water. "I know the poaching isn't as bad here as it is on the Caribbean side, but the more visitors you have, the more people will be walking the beach, and the safer the turtle eggs will be."

"Volunteers sometimes give donations too," Zo-Zo said. "The Wild Place gets lots of money that way."

Griff shrugged. "I wouldn't say *lots,* but still —"

Carlos's eyes inflated like party balloons. "Always need money."

"We should make a video!" Squirm began juggling two spoons in the air. "People *love* videos! We could put it right on the site!"

Zo-Zo smiled at Carlos. "You'd be the star. We could show you doing patrols, collecting eggs, maybe releasing baby turtles …"

Carlos blushed, but Robin could tell he liked the idea.

Squirm was now working the spoons like drum sticks, tapping out a rhythm on the table. "Maybe I could put some of my insect pictures on the site."

"Good idea," Carlos said. "Let's fix website, but collect eggs too. I want hatchery full."

"Full," Robin repeated. "How many eggs would make it full?"

"Have one hundred now," Carlos said, calculating. His face brightened. "A thousand?"

"Let's go for it," Zo-Zo cried.

"A thousand," Griff said. "You sure? That's a *lot* of eggs."

"We can do it," Robin said, her tone full of resolve.

"Fine for you to say," Squirm quipped. "You'll be on the computer."

"Just for a few days," Robin said. "I'll start on the website while my foot's getting better, then come and help with the eggs."

Griff nodded. "Maybe Squirm and I can start by taking pictures for the site. The grounds, kitchen, dorm, hatchery. Just to give people a sense of the place."

Zo-Zo grabbed a pencil. "And I can work with Carlos to write what he wants the website to say." She waved him over to another table.

Robin got the admin details from Carlos and pulled the site up. She started by uploading a large picture of a leatherback and putting it right at the top of the page, then she superimposed the words *The Playa Tortuguitas Sanctuary* on top of it. She put the Spanish name underneath.

All afternoon, Griff kept bringing her photographs of the sanctuary. Robin knew how important pictures were, so she showed pictures of the egg hatchery, Benita cooking a meal, Marcos holding a huge leatherback shell, and lots of photos of leatherbacks.

Midway through the afternoon, Squirm gave her several beautiful pictures of the flowers and birds and butterflies they'd seen on their forest walk. He also gave her photographs of other animals that visitors might see: black iguanas, howler monkeys, hairy dwarf porcupines, white-throated magpie-jays, grackles, kiskadees, and trogons.

"I love that name, *trogon*," Squirm said. "Sounds like something out of Harry Potter."

Robin smiled and uploaded the pictures to the site.

In the late afternoon, Zo-Zo brought her the written description she'd been working on with Carlos, and Robin arranged the words around the pictures. When she was done, she called everyone around to look.

"Wow. Cool," Squirm said. "Very cool."

Griff clapped her hands. "Well done, girl. Well done!" She made a few suggestions, including the idea of highlighting the words *Visitors Welcome,* so Robin put a bright-red box around the words to make sure they stood out. She also added the turtle sanctuary's email address and a button that said *Contact Now.*

Carlos looked at it and couldn't stop smiling. "*Pura vida,*" he said over and over.

Robin knew he was pleased, and she continued to work on the site after dinner as well.

Some time in the evening, Zo-Zo appeared beside her. She had arranged her hair in dozens of little braids to keep it off her face and had an elastic around the back of her glasses to keep them from sliding down her nose in the heat.

"Carlos just did a quick walk on the beach while we were working on the website and found some eggs," Zo-Zo said. "He and Diego are relocating them in the hatchery. I'm going to take some pictures." She grabbed her phone. "Then we're all heading out on patrol," she said as she breezed out of the room.

Robin hobbled over to the window and watched as the two men finished the relocation. They were just smoothing the sand over the spot, and Zo-Zo was taking pictures. When they were done, Diego went back to his deck chair and sat down. Griff and Squirm appeared and waved at Robin as they headed along the beach with Zo-Zo and Carlos.

Robin wished she could join them, but her foot was hurting from just her short walk to the window. There was no way.

Wanting to be productive despite her inactivity, she worked on the website for a while, but her foot really began to throb. She took one of the pills Griff had left her, turned off the lights, and went to bed.

As she lay under the light cotton sheet, she stared out the window, waiting for the pain in her toe to ease. The moon was out, and even though it was only half full, it was bright enough to light up the turtle hatchery outside.

She saw someone wandering around inside the fence. Diego. Keeping hidden, she straightened up so she could see him better and watched as he walked over to the area where she'd seen him and Carlos earlier. To her surprise, when he reached the spot where he and Carlos had relocated the eggs, he bent down and started to dig with a small shovel.

She tensed. Dig? Why was he digging? Then she saw a turtle egg in his hand. Turning his head one way and then the other as if to make sure he wasn't being watched, he hid the egg in a bag and dug for another.

Robin counted as he put the stolen eggs in the bag. There were twenty.

He stopped digging, set the bag aside, and began pushing the sand back into the hole, taking time to smooth over the top again so it didn't look as if the ground had been disturbed.

Taking a furtive look around and not seeing anyone, he wandered out to the lane.

He was out of view now, so Robin got out of bed and stealthily shuffled through the dark dormitory and into the dining area, hoping to continue watching him.

By the time she was able to see him again, he was out by the road. He whistled softly as if to someone who might be waiting. A few minutes later, a man with a limp approached. Diego handed the man the bag of turtle eggs.

"Stop!" Robin heard the word erupt into the quiet and expected him to look up, but he didn't. She'd shouted only in her mind.

The man with a limp put the bag of turtle eggs on the ground and pulled two bottles from the side pockets of his shirt. Diego took them and hurried away. When the man was out of sight, Diego opened one of the bottles, took a swig, and walked over to a small shed. There, he pulled back a piece of the siding and arranged the bottles in a little cubbyhole. Whistling ever so softly, he returned to his chair.

Robin scuttled back to bed as fast as she could and pulled the sheet over her. It was hot in the room, but her bones felt as cold as icicles.

CHAPTER
ELEVEN

Robin didn't know what time it was when the commotion woke her. Dark shadows of people came running in, hands found her, shook her, pulled her out of the bed. She was alarmed until she heard giggles.

Giggles? She relaxed.

"Robin! Get up! We want to show you something."

Was that Zo-Zo? It sounded like her, but Robin felt groggy and couldn't tell for sure.

Someone flicked a switch, and suddenly the room exploded with light. Squirm, Zo-Zo, and Carlos were all grinning at her, their faces bursting with glee.

Robin sat up. *Diego. The turtle eggs.* She had to tell them what she'd seen, she had to te—

Zo-Zo yanked at her arm. "Come on. We want to take you up the beach."

"I can't, my foot, I ..." There was no way she could walk the beach. Besides, what was the point of finding eggs if Diego was selling them? What was the point of even being here, doing the website, doing anything, if Diego was just going to sabotage all their good efforts?

No, she had to tell the others what he had done.

But what if Diego was listening? She looked out into the black night. For all she knew, he could have his ear pressed against the wall beside her window right now. That could make talking dangerous. She forced herself to keep quiet until she found her grandmother. The moment she did, she'd pull her into a private corner and tell her the whole terrible story.

"Where's Griff?"

"Waiting for you," Zo-Zo said. "A little way up the beach."

Robin pressed her lips together and rolled them back into her mouth. She felt as if she were going to explode.

Squirm wiggled with excitement. "You've got to see this."

Laughing, Zo-Zo waved Carlos forward, and they each took one of Robin's arms and draped it over a shoulder.

"Stand on one foot," Zo-Zo said. When Robin did, Zo-Zo and Carlos lifted her up.

"Walk on good leg," Carlos said, and Robin did as he instructed. Soon she was peg-legging it along the beach, digging her good foot into the sand every second step her friends took and swinging along in between. Thus, they sped along the beach into the blackness.

It's like having crutches, she thought. *Human ones.*

Squirm ran along beside them.

At first it was so dark, Robin could only hear the waves, but slowly, as her eyes adjusted, she could see the white curl of the surf splashing on shore. After several minutes, Carlos and Zo-Zo slowed their pace.

"Shh!" Squirm said.

They were creeping along now. Robin could hear something going *swish, swish, swish* up ahead.

Her eyes bored into the darkness as she searched for what was making that sound. Then she saw it. A massive leatherback.

Griff appeared at Robin's side. "She's huge," she whispered.

"Sometime called *baúl* in Spanish," Carlos said in a hushed voice. "Means 'big trunk.'"

Robin could see why. The leatherback was almost as big as an ATV.

The turtle stopped moving forward and started using her flippers to dig a hole in the sand. On and on she dug, until the hole was about seventy-five centimetres deep.

Robin stared at the turtle, utterly transfixed. Everything that had happened earlier in the evening seemed to fall away. It was as if she'd been transported back a few million years and was seeing an animal as ancient as time itself. Its primal magnificence awed her.

"Look!" Squirm shrieked in a muffled whisper. "Eggs!"

Robin kneeled and bent her head down until she could see the eggs dropping out of the turtle's body into the pit. The eggs were as big as snowballs and just as white.

"Can I put on my flashlight?" Squirm asked.

Carlos and Griff shook their heads at the same time.

Griff smiled with understanding. "Let's not invade her privacy any more than we already have."

The eggs kept coming and coming. When there were no more, the leatherback used her back flippers to cover the eggs and compact the sand, making the nest indistinguishable from the rest of the beach. Finished now, she slowly hunkered her way back to the ocean.

"Bye," Squirm said quietly as they watched her disappear into the waves.

"We'll keep your babies safe," Robin said, staring out into the ocean. It felt like a huge responsibility.

Carlos pulled on some thin plastic gloves and began burrowing into the sand with his hands.

"Can we help?" Robin asked.

He gave them all rubber gloves, and they set to work digging out the hole.

Robin used her fingers as scoops. The sand on the top was granular and easy to shift, but it got wetter and harder to move the farther down she went. She slowed her hands when she got to where she thought the eggs would be.

"Shells still soft," Carlos said. "Gentle to not damage."

Robin worked even more carefully now. Finally, she felt something smooth and curvy and coaxed an egg out of the sand. She made a basket out of her hands and held the egg to her chest. She felt as excited as if she were holding a hunk of gold. It might just be her imagination, she thought, but she was sure she could feel the aliveness of the baby inside. How magical was that?

Carlos pulled some bags from his knapsack. "Special for moving eggs," he said. "Clean. Very clean."

Using great caution, they began loading the eggs into the bags. When they had collected every last one, Robin sat back on her heels. If her toe hurt, she wasn't aware of it. Her entire body was thrumming with deep satisfaction. Diego might have diminished the turtle sanctuary's egg supply earlier that night, but what they'd done now would make up for that.

When all the eggs were packed into the bags, Squirm and Griff hoisted them up and started to head back. Once they were on their way, Carlos and Zo-Zo arranged Robin like before and followed behind.

As they approached the hatchery, Robin could smell the smoke from Diego's cigarette. When she was closer, she could see him sitting in a deck chair at the edge of the hatchery. She had to pass him to go into it and was sure she could smell alcohol. Carlos must have smelled it too, for he spoke harshly to Diego in Spanish. Then he turned to them.

"Go to bed," he said. "I take care of eggs."

Robin was grateful. She didn't want to be anywhere near Diego. She looked around for Griff. Robin found her already in bed, sound asleep.

She made a promise to herself. First thing tomorrow morning, she'd ask Griff to go for a walk and tell her what Diego had done. Yawning, she hopped over to her bed and almost fell on the mattress. Too exhausted even to change into her pajamas, she fell asleep in her clothes.

CHAPTER
TWELVE

Robin was running up the beach, her lungs desperately grabbing air as her legs pumped and pumped. Someone was chasing her. She had to get away. Before they caught her. Before they —

She wrenched herself from the dream and opened her eyes. *What the …?* She blinked, trying to reorient herself. Where *was* she? Nothing in her surroundings looked familiar. Then she saw Squirm and Zo-Zo sleeping in the other beds and remembered. She was in Costa Rica. At a turtle sanctuary. And she'd just had a nightmare.

If only what she'd seen Diego do last night had been a nightmare too. But it was real and replayed in her mind now as if it had happened only moments ago. A scared feeling clenched her stomach and wouldn't let go.

She sat up. She was going to search out Griff right now and pour out all the grim details. Griff would know what to do.

She peeked out the window. Diego was in his usual spot, sitting under a tree at the edge of the hatchery. He looked over at her, and she flinched, darting away from view. Did he suspect that she'd seen him last night?

She shivered and walked into the dining area. Her foot wasn't so sore now — that was good — but she felt tense. The sooner she saw her grandmother, the better she was going to feel.

Benita waved at her from the kitchen.

Robin didn't wave back. "Where's Griff?"

Benita pointed toward the beach. "She, Carlos, walking." She slid a bowl of mangoes and papayas along the counter.

Too agitated to eat, Robin left the fruit bowl untouched and slumped down in the chair near the computer. She brought the new turtle sanctuary website onto her screen.

The pictures and stories they'd added the day before looked good. Really good. There was even an email. Surprised, she opened it. It was from a girl in England asking if turtles could breathe underwater.

Robin smiled and felt her tension ease. She'd let Carlos answer the girl's inquiry, but it felt good to think that because of the new website, people from other parts of the world were learning about turtles and the turtle sanctuary. Maybe some of them would decide to come and visit one day. And if they did, they might get to see a leatherback nesting, like she had last night. There was something about seeing a real live animal up close like that. It changed a person. No one could experience that and not want to help. Somehow, she had to bring more people here so that could happen.

She was enlarging one of the pictures when Marcos wandered by, banana in hand. He went into the dorm area and a few minutes later, reappeared with Squirm, who was carrying a notebook and a magnifying glass.

Squirm grabbed a papaya from the bowl on the table and stuffed it into the pocket of his shorts. "We're going hunting for Hercules beetles." He waved and the two of them went off.

Robin was putting a caption below one of the pictures when another email came in. Something tingled in her knees as she read it. She read it again. A light, happy feeling washed over her, sloshing everything else out of her mind.

Hearing Griff and Carlos come in from the beach, she called them over.

"Hey! We just got an email from some church group in Texas. They want to know if we take visitors."

Carlos stared at her quizzically, as if she was speaking a language he'd never heard before.

"That's exciting news." Griff tilted back her water bottle and took a long drink as Robin continued.

"They know it's last minute, but some trip they'd booked got cancelled, so they want to know if they can come here." She looked at Carlos and waved to Zo-Zo, who had just come in the room.

"Hey, Zo! Guess what? Some people want to book a visit!"

Zo-Zo's eyes widened. "Visit, as in *pay* to visit?"

"If they were going to pay for a trip somewhere else, I'm sure they'll pay us," Griff said, looking at Carlos. "That will help pay the bills."

Robin felt exuberant. This was the best thing that could have happened. "Think of all the help we'll get collecting eggs," she said.

"We might even make our goal of a thousand," Zo-Zo added. "How long do they want to come for?"

Robin raced through the email again. "Five days."

"And how many people?" Griff asked.

"Eight."

Carlos looked doubtful. "No place put."

"Oh, Carlos," Griff said. "Surely you don't want to turn away paying guests because of 'No place put.' Think of the things you could do with the money! You could buy supplies, put a better fence around the hatchery, paint the place …"

Carlos still looked skeptical.

"And once they see the leatherbacks, they'll want to protect them forever," Robin cried.

Carlos threw his hands up. "Where sleep?"

Griff tossed her long white braid over her shoulder. "We could give them the dormitory if we had to. And sleep outside."

"Problem," Carlos said. "Only four beds in dorm."

"Tents," Robin cried. "We could get tents."

Carlos frowned. "Cost money, tents."

"There's no problem a little imagination can't solve," Griff said. She leaned over Robin's shoulder and started typing an email. "I'll ask Finn if he'll buy some tents. He's already said he wants to help."

"Awesome!" Zo-Zo shot a victory fist into the air. "Finn's awesome."

He is *awesome*, Robin thought. Finn's first love might be whales, but as she'd learned on the whaling expedition, he was a sucker for all types of animals. He was just that kind of guy. No wonder Griff adored him.

"Who is this Finn?" Carlos wanted to know.

"He saves whales." Robin googled Finn's name and showed Carlos some photos of him and his adventures.

Carlos whistled his admiration.

"We went to Antarctica with him," Zo-Zo said. "He'll say yes to the tents, I know he will."

While they waited for Finn to reply, Robin and Zo-Zo spent the next few hours researching places in Costa Rica where they could buy tents. They had their options narrowed down to two when Griff's phone pinged.

Robin knew from the warmth that blossomed on her grandmother's face that the text was from Finn.

"Says he'll donate the money for four tents," Griff said, reading the text aloud. Her smile got bigger and bigger. "Four tents and eight cots."

Robin and Zo-Zo gave each other a high-five. Robin turned to Carlos.

"So I can tell the church group to come?"

He nodded solemnly.

"You'll need to quote them a price," Griff said. "What do you think, Carlos? What do you want to charge?"

Carlos shrugged and said an amount of money.

The lines on Griff's face seemed to tangle. She raised her voice. "For meals, accommodation, tours, and lectures? I don't think so!" She turned her head toward Robin. "Double that amount. Let's see what they say."

Robin wrote back to the Texas group, sending them more photographs of leatherback turtles, as well as a few of the sanctuary and some of the wildlife they'd seen the other day in the forest.

When Robin finished, it was late afternoon. She realized she'd forgotten to tell Griff about Diego. She still wanted to do it, but it didn't seem as pressing now. Still, she knew it was necessary, so she went in search of her grandmother, only to learn that Griff had gone into the village to get some groceries. While she was gone, a delivery truck pulled up, and a man got out and handed Robin her lost piece of luggage.

Pleased to see her things, Robin spent the next hour organizing her stuff. She pulled out a pair of shorts that was in the bag and when she put her hands into the pockets, the fingers of her left hand came upon something. She pulled it out.

It was the acorn Griff had given her all those months ago.

Ha!

She rolled it in her hand, then went in search of Griff. She found her helping Benita with dinner and thought about calling her aside, but decided to do it later, when they were out on the beach. Robin's foot was better now, and she was planning on going on patrol. That would give her the perfect opportunity to talk privately with Griff.

As soon as they all started walking, however, they came across a leatherback pulling herself out of the water and looking for a place to lay her eggs. The next few hours were spent waiting for the leatherback to dig her nest. Then, since the nest was a large one, it took them a few hours to gather up all the eggs, bag them, and bring them back to the hatchery. By the time they had the eggs buried in the sand back at the sanctuary, Robin was exhausted.

Griff was obviously exhausted too, because when Robin came into the dorm, her grandmother was already snoring soundly. Robin had missed her opportunity again.

Needing to tell someone, she pushed her bed beside Zo-Zo's, and after they'd turned the lights out, whispered what she'd seen Diego do.

"That's *terrible*," Zo-Zo said. "Have you told Griff?"

"Not yet. But I will."

"He's just going to deny it," Zo-Zo said. "It will be your word against his."

"Griff will believe me," Robin asserted. Of that she was certain.

"Yeah, but will Carlos?" Zo-Zo asked. "Wait. Wait until you can prove it."

Prove it? How the heck was she going to do that?

CHAPTER THIRTEEN

The next day was the busiest day yet. It started with an email from the church group saying that they were coming. In a week. The news was like a gun firing at a starting gate, causing them all to charge into action. There was so much to do.

They made a long list and started with the most important thing: figuring out where the eight people of the church group were going to sleep. Robin and Zo-Zo spent more time researching options, and when they finally zeroed in on a place that sold decent tents and cots at a price Griff thought they could afford, they had to spend an entire day driving there with Carlos, buying everything, and bringing it all back.

The day after that was spent clearing the sites where the tents were going to go. They had to make sure the ground was flat and didn't have any stones or roots protruding, so they raked and raked until it was perfect.

When they had the four sites ready, Carlos pulled one of the canvas tents from the long box, and they all stared at the heap of poles and nets and zippers. Carlos scratched his head as he studied the Spanish instructions. Squirm ran and got his Spanish-English dictionary, but finally they tossed the instructions aside and assembled one through trial and error. It took them hours.

The second tent went up more quickly, and by the time they erected the fourth tent, it took just over a half an hour.

The cots were easier to put together, because they only had to screw some long metal pipes into each other, then push them down long fabric inserts that made up the sides of the cots. Once they had the bed part of the cot together, all they had to do was connect the pipes that acted as legs. It still took them a long time.

Squirm lay down on one of the cots when they were finished. "Not bad," he said. "All I need is a pillow and a sleeping bag."

"The church group is bringing those," Robin told him. Griff had suggested this, and Robin was glad she had. It was one less thing to think about. And she already had about a hundred others on her mind. What were they going to feed them? How were they going to handle all the dishes? What about showers? Lectures? Beach walks?

With all these details yelling at her for attention, the oath that she started every day with, to tell Griff about Diego, simply slipped into the background. And she let it. Maybe the incident with Diego was just a one-off deal. Maybe it would never happen again. These were the excuses she told herself, but in truth, she was afraid of Diego. Afraid of what he'd do if she told. So she allowed herself not to think about it and concentrated on what she had to do to get ready for the church group.

Once the tents and cots were all in place, they turned their attention to cleaning the place up. Robin remembered how rundown it had looked when they'd first arrived, and she didn't want the church group thinking the place was a dump.

It wasn't that it was dirty. Benita made sure of that, but it looked scruffy somehow. Even after Robin spent the whole day washing walls and clearing things away, the place still looked dingy.

"Maybe we should paint it," Robin suggested.

"We don't have time," Griff said.

"Three days," Robin countered. "We can do a lot in three days."

"Yeah!" Squirm squealed. "Let's paint it jujube orange. I *love* that colour."

"No, red," Zo-Zo cried. "We should paint it red. Fire-engine red."

Suddenly, Carlos called from the hatchery, interrupting them. "*Bebés*. Come. *Bebés* hatching."

They all flew outside and huddled around one of the nests. The same nest Robin had seen Diego marauding.

"Whoa," Squirm said as he stared down at it. "The sand has all caved in."

Robin stared too. Not only had the nest collapsed in on itself, there was a lot of commotion going on. The sand itself looked as if it were bubbling up from within.

"Eggs breaking," Carlos said. "*Bebés* coming out."

Something black jutted up to the surface. It looked like a tiny head. It *was* a tiny head. Then tiny arms appeared, and a tiny shell, and finally, a small turtle was standing on the top of the sand pile.

"Awww ..."

Robin felt as if her heart had turned into warm honey.

Zo-Zo and Squirm crooned beside her as other little noses appeared. Soon there were dozens of tiny bodies scurrying around on the sand, bumping into each other and climbing over each other's shells.

"They're looking for the ocean," Griff said.

Carlos grabbed a box. "Put here." With expert speed, he began catching the babies.

Robin picked up one of the turtles. It wasn't much bigger than a loonie. It flailed its tiny legs as she lifted it up.

"It's okay," she whispered. "You're going to the ocean."

Beside her, Carlos pulled out the popsicle-shaped stick that marked the nest. It had the date and the number of eggs written on it. She glanced at the number. It said *100*. She knew that of the original hundred eggs, only about half would have hatched into baby turtles. Which meant there should have been about fifty hatchlings. And there would have been. If Diego hadn't made his raid.

She stuffed the stick that Carlos had put down into the pocket of her shorts and continued catching babies and putting them in the box.

When they had gathered up every last turtle, Carlos shut the lid of the box and carried it down to the beach. He took it to the same area where the nest had been originally found.

Robin followed. She looked back, relieved to see that Diego had resumed his spot in his chair and was not coming with them.

When they arrived at the right spot, Carlos opened the box and was just about to turn it over and release the turtles when Robin said, "Count them."

He shrugged but did as she suggested, taking one turtle out at a time and counting in English. "One, two, three, four …"

As the turtles were set on the sand, Robin couldn't tell whether they smelled or heard the ocean, but they definitely knew the ocean was close, for they raced toward it like toddlers to their mother.

"Look at them." Zo-Zo grinned as she watched the babies scurrying across the sand. "Aren't they adorable?"

"Beyond adorable," Griff said as she took pictures with her phone. Squirm was beside her taking a video. They wanted to capture every moment of the release for the website.

Carlos continued to count the turtles as he set them on the sand. "Twelve, thirteen …"

Robin looked at the turtles remaining in the box and ran through the numbers again. There should have been about fifty hatchlings. But she could see from the number remaining in the box that there weren't that many.

"Sixteen, seventeen …"

One of the hatchlings got flipped over on its back. Robin reached forward, picked it up, and set it on its feet again.

"And now the last one," Carlos said as he set it on the sand. He looked confused as he said the number aloud. "Twenty." He looked up at Robin. "No more?"

Robin shook her head, pulled the stick out of her pocket, and gave it to him.

"Must wrote wrong," he said, looking troubled.

Robin felt herself freeze. She could barely breathe. It was just like that day up in the attic with the raccoons. She felt immobilized, unable to move. Griff's words came back to her. *Robin, think about the babies. Think about the babies.*

So she thought about the baby turtles. The ones Diego had taken. The ones that would never run along the beach or swim in the ocean because of Diego. Her fury rose, overriding her fear.

She straightened her body and spoke. Her voice sounded strong and determined.

"The number on the marker is right," she said. "Diego stole the other eggs and sold them for liquor. I saw him."

CHAPTER
FOURTEEN

Robin told the whole story to Carlos while the others listened, too stunned to say anything.

When she was done, Griff rubbed her jaw with her large hand and murmured, "Oh, Robin, I wish you'd told me."

They walked back to the sanctuary, and when they got there, Carlos told Griff and the kids to stay inside while he went to confront Diego.

Griff grabbed his arm as he was going out, her voice fierce. "Don't tell him that Robin was the one to blow the whistle. That could be dangerous for her. I don't want her put at risk."

Robin swallowed hard. It didn't matter whether Carlos said her name or not. Diego would know. She could *feel* it.

"I have *own* proof," Carlos said, holding up the marker from the robbed nest. "Number here and number of babies not same." He shook his head angrily and went out.

Robin and the others positioned themselves by the window so they could watch. Robin felt Squirm nuzzling into her nervously, and she had to remind herself to breathe.

They watched as Carlos strode over to Diego, and the two men began to talk. There wasn't much to see, but the escalating sound made up for the lack of visuals. Within minutes, the two men were shouting at each other.

Robin tugged at Griff's T-shirt. "What are they saying, Griff? What are they saying?"

"Just what you'd expect. Diego says he didn't steal the eggs. And swears he's not drinking, and Carlos is accusing him of doing both those things."

Carlos held up the marker stick, and the voices got louder still. Finally, Carlos strode toward the shed where Robin had told him Diego had stashed the bottles. Robin held her breath. She had hoped Carlos wouldn't have to show this part. If there was anything that might give her away, it was that.

Carlos pulled the two bottles out and uncapped each of them, sniffing the contents. Then he turned the bottles upside down. One was empty, but the second bottle spewed the dregs of some brown liquid.

Griff continued to translate. "Now Carlos is telling him to pack up his stuff. Says he's going to drive him to the bus station."

Robin stared at Diego. His face was swollen with rage as he shouted down the pathway that led to the house where he stayed.

"Benita!"

Almost immediately, Benita appeared, Marcos close as a shadow behind her.

Griff carried on translating. "Diego's telling her to pack up. He's saying Carlos is kicking them off the property. Because someone told lies about him."

"Lies!" Robin hissed indignantly. *They weren't lies!* Was Benita going to believe him?

Loud, agitated words erupted out of Benita.

"Whoa!" Squirm whispered beside Robin. "She sure sounds *mad!*"

Diego grabbed Benita's arm roughly and tried to pull her toward their house, but she wrenched herself from his grip.

Robin heard the breath catch in her grandmother's throat. "Good for you, Benita. Good for you."

Robin again tugged on Griff's sleeve. "What's she saying? What's she saying?"

"She's saying that she's not going to go with him. She's saying she doesn't want to live with a drunk."

"I wouldn't want to hang around Diego even if he wasn't a drunk," Zo-Zo said.

Benita ran toward the kitchen, her face contorted with hurt and anger. Within seconds she was inside. She turned, and Marcos hid his face in his mother's chest. Griff put her arms protectively around them both.

Robin stood rigidly on red alert. Was Diego going to storm inside now too? She listened hard, waiting for any sound that would tell her to start running. But the only sound was Marcos's muffled snuffling as he cried.

When someone did come in, it was Carlos. He grabbed his van keys. "I take Diego to bus. He go to brother in other town." He said something to Benita, but she shook her head vehemently. There was no way she was joining her husband.

While Carlos was gone, Benita busied herself in the kitchen, and the rest of them sat around one of the tables, unsure of what to do next. Robin felt relieved that Diego had gone, but she felt jangled somehow, stuck. As if all the shouted words were still around her, strewn over the floor like treacherous bits of broken glass.

There were only a few days until the church group would be there, and Robin knew she should get to the many things that needed doing, but she felt too discombobulated to concentrate.

"I sure hope he doesn't come back," Squirm said.

Everyone nodded in solemn agreement.

Griff looked around at their sombre faces. "So, how do we put this situation behind us and go forward?"

Go forward? How the heck were they going to do that? Robin wondered. Everything felt tainted somehow. Ruined. She wracked her brain for something that might radically change the feeling.

Her mind wandered back to the time they'd moved into the farmhouse from Winnipeg. Her dad had painted her bedroom, and with each stroke of the sun-yellow paint, the room had been transformed. That's what they needed now. A transformation. Something to lift their spirits before the church group came.

"Let's paint the place," she said. She had wanted to do that a few days ago, and now she wanted to more than ever.

Squirm's face brightened. "Yeah!" He pulled an orange jujube out of his pocket. "I like this colour."

"No way," Zo-Zo argued.

Griff held her hand up like a stop sign. "I've had enough conflict for one day, thank you very much."

Benita appeared and put a cup of tea in front of Griff. Coffee was the traditional drink in Costa Rica, but Benita knew how much Griff loved tea.

Griff smiled up at her. "Such kindness." She took a grateful sip. "You remember this, kids. Kindness is like a candle in the dark. It goes a long way in difficult moments."

Benita went back into the kitchen, and Griff sipped her tea. "I think I saw some paint at the local store. Nothing fancy. Just colours like red, green, yellow, blue. But a bit of colour would really jazz this place up."

"Let's do it," Squirm cried.

"I'll call Carlos on his cell. See what he thinks," Griff said, taking her tea and moving to the far side of the room to make the call. She came back smiling.

"Carlos said he can pick up the paint on the way back. I told him to get a few tins of everything — red, yellow, and blue."

Squirm turned to Robin. "You can make orange by putting red and yellow together, right?"

Robin laughed and started pushing the benches into the centre of the room. *Transformation, here we come.*

CHAPTER FIFTEEN

The night before the group was to arrive, Robin and the others walked through the rooms of the sanctuary, admiring the kaleidoscope of colour. The kitchen was red, the dining area was yellow, the dormitory was orange — jujube orange — and the building itself was light blue.

Zo-Zo twirled in delight. "It's awesome! *Way* better than before."

Squirm had splatters of paint all over his clothes, as well as his skin. "I knew it was going to look like a rainbow," he said.

"You're the one who looks like a rainbow." Griff smiled.

Carlos wandered through the sanctuary as if he'd been transported to a different planet.

Robin pulled him outside. There was something she wanted to show him.

"Look," she said, pointing to the main door. On it she'd stencilled a bunch of turtles. "Just like the ones tattooed on your arm."

Carlos grinned. Robin had never seen him so happy.

Benita called from the kitchen. When they all went

inside, she began cutting big slices of a cake she'd just baked. She'd been baking some special things for the church group and wanted to try them out on the kids.

"Lemon cake," Squirm said. "Yum."

Robin was still full from dinner, but the cake was so good she ate a whole piece anyway. Squirm had two pieces. Then they all went out on patrol.

Since there was no one to guard the eggs, Carlos put a big padlock at the front of the hatchery gate, then said he was coming on patrol with them.

"Just for first minutes," he said.

Robin could tell he was nervous about leaving the hatchery unguarded, but she also knew he couldn't resist coming on patrol. At least for a little while. They would probably do a very short one tonight.

When they started walking on the beach, there was no moon and it was dark. Robin felt apprehensive. What if Diego wasn't hundreds of kilometres away like they all thought he was? What if he'd jumped off the bus at the first stop from the station and had walked back and was hiding in the bushes somewhere, just waiting for a chance to get his revenge?

Stop, she told herself. *Stop.* But she was tired, and when she was tired, it was harder to control what went on in her mind. Unwanted, scary thoughts kept scuttling into her brain like bugs that ran into the open when the lights went out.

Carlos stayed with them for the first hour, then jogged back to the hatchery. The rest of them walked for another hour, but they didn't find any nests that night and came back early.

Since the church group would be there first thing in the morning, they all went to bed. Robin expected to fall asleep immediately, but couldn't. There were too many things swirling around in her head. What if the church group was a bunch of old fuddy-duddies with nothing good to say about anything? What if it rained all day and people couldn't go out on the beach? What if there wasn't a turtle nest to be found when the group had their hearts set on seeing one?

Around and around these thoughts went, and just when she was certain she wasn't going to sleep at all, Griff shook her.

"Come on, sleepyhead. They'll be here in fifteen minutes."

Robin pulled herself up. She had just finished getting dressed when she heard the group chattering as they got off the bus. Suppressing a yawn, she went out to welcome them.

The next few hours, Robin and everyone else helped carry bags and get people settled. She was bombarded with questions. A woman with red hair asked her if leatherbacks really were on the verge of extinction, a man with a dolphin on his T-shirt asked if leatherbacks returned to the same beach where they were born to lay their eggs, and a woman with her hair in a ponytail asked her why leatherbacks had rubbery rather than hard shells.

Once everyone had been given a bed, Carlos and Marcos took the group on a walk through the forest. After that, Carlos gave a talk on leatherbacks. He showed slides and Griff translated when necessary.

During the show, Robin noticed a little girl with

curly hair clinging to her father. Her head was turned away from the screen. When the slide show was finished, Robin went over to them.

The man extended his hand. "I'm Richard Hughes. And this is Lola."

Robin stared at the little girl. She was about six and had white-blonde hair. She wouldn't look at Robin, pretending instead to be engrossed in fiddling with her father's expensive watch. She did not look happy.

Mr. Hughes explained. "Lola was bitten by a snapping turtle last year. Now she won't go near any kind of turtle. I was hoping this trip might help her to be less afraid."

Robin lifted her foot and wiggled her toe at Lola. "I got stung by a scorpion a few weeks ago. Right on my toe. Want to see?"

Lola took a suspicious glance at Robin's out-stretched leg.

Robin lifted her foot higher. "See the sting mark on the end of my big toe?"

Lola peered forward. "Did it hurt?"

"Big time," Robin said.

Lola kicked off a flip-flop and raised her foot so it was right in front of Robin's eyes.

Robin could see a slight mark on the end of Lola's toe. "Wow. That turtle took a chunk out of you, didn't he?" She looked into the little girl's eyes. "Snapping turtles don't usually bite. He must have thought your toe was a marshmallow or something. It looks a bit like a marsh-mallow, don't you think?"

Lola smiled ever so slightly, and Mr. Hughes gave Robin a grateful look.

Around them the rest of the group started to move in preparation for a beach walk.

"We're going out to look for turtles," Robin said. "You coming?"

Lola shook her head vehemently.

Mr. Hughes sighed. "Now it's not just turtles she wants to avoid, it's the beach they might be walking on."

Robin wanted to stay and talk more, but she had promised Carlos she'd be on hand to answer questions during the beach walk, so she waved goodbye and headed out with the others.

At first there were lots of questions, but soon the sun and wind and waves seemed to relax everyone, and the people in the group got quieter and quieter, enjoying the beauty around them.

On the way back, Griff walked along beside her.

"That poor little girl," Griff said.

"Lola?"

Griff nodded. "I heard you talking to her and her dad." She shrugged. "Being bitten by a turtle must have been scary. She's probably replayed it in her mind a thousand times. It's not going to be easy to get that memory out. Let's just hope she doesn't try to avoid turtles for the rest of her life. And beaches too."

"That would be sad," Robin said.

"I know, but people don't think straight when they're afraid," Griff said.

Robin thought about that. It was true. Her brain seemed to go fuzzy when she was fearful. Like that day up in the attic.

"Isn't there anything we can do?" she asked Griff.

Her grandmother was pensive. "Let's just try to give her as many good experiences with turtles as we can. See if we can settle that fear of hers down."

Robin thought about that for the rest of the walk. When they were on their way back, she saw a small ridley turtle and picked it up.

Back at the sanctuary, Robin found Lola and her dad playing cards in the main room. Robin sat at the table beside them and set the turtle down.

The turtle looked up at them but did not move.

"It looks scared," Robin said.

Lola's eyes widened. "Scared of us?"

"We must look like giants to this little guy," Robin said.

Lola seemed surprised by the idea that the turtle might be afraid, and she stared at it for a long while. The longer she stared, the more evident it became to her that there was nothing to be afraid of. When Robin saw Lola beginning to relax, she took the turtle back to the beach.

Every day, Robin brought a turtle for Lola to look at. Each time she did, Lola reacted at first, but then became less afraid. She still wouldn't go out on the beach, but Robin got the feeling that she might soon.

The rest of the church group went out on the beach all the time. Nearly all of them took part in the nightly nest-finding patrol, even though it meant hours of walking. As a result, there were many more encounters with nesting turtles, and the number of eggs in the hatchery climbed steadily.

Wanting to show the group their progress, Robin made a big thermometer poster out of cardboard and wrote *1,000 EGGS* at the top and *0* at the bottom. She drew a line at *410*, which was the number of eggs they'd relocated so far, and coloured in the thermometer to that number. They were almost halfway to their goal!

She was pinning the poster to one of the walls in the dining area as everyone was finishing lunch when Mr. Hughes asked her about the egg-collecting project.

"When we go back to Canada," Robin explained, "we want to leave a thousand eggs in the hatchery. If we do that, the leatherbacks will have a chance of surviving. At least for a while."

"That's very impressive, young lady," he said. He was pensive for a long moment. "Tell you what. I'm a businessman, and in my company we always offer incentives. So I'm going to offer you one. I'll give the sanctuary a thousand dollars if you collect a thousand eggs. Not by the time we leave, but by the time *you* leave."

Robin whistled. A thousand dollars! The turtle sanctuary would be able to do a lot with a thousand dollars.

Squirm called over to Zo-Zo. "Did you hear that? He's going to give us a thousand dollars if we collect a thousand eggs."

Zo-Zo shot a victory fist into the air.

Griff came over, and so did Carlos, who pumped Mr. Hughes's hand with great enthusiasm.

When the other members of the church group found out about Mr. Hughes's offer, they worked even harder to find nests. Some of the group, however, weren't as interested in nests as they were in seeing hatchlings. Carlos had told them that some of the eggs were due to hatch any day, and everyone was hoping that this would happen before the church group headed for home.

"You can't rush Mother Nature," Griff kept telling everyone.

Her advice was proving to be true, for the days passed and there was no sign that any baby turtles were about to appear.

The day before the group was due to leave, they were beginning to pack up and getting ready to make the long bus ride to the airport when Carlos started shouting.

"*Bebés! Bebés!*"

Everyone ran outside. To protect the other nests from being stepped on, Carlos wanted only a few people in the enclosure area, but Robin asked him especially if Mr. Hughes and Lola could come in. He agreed, so Robin waved them through the gate.

One of the nests was a chaos of motion. Soon a baby turtle clawed its way to the surface. Others followed. Within minutes, dozens of them were scuttling across the sand. They were so tiny and adorable that Robin wasn't surprised to see Lola watching them with fascination.

Robin and Carlos began to gather the babies up, putting them into a box for transport to the beach.

"Want to see the babies run to the ocean?" Robin asked Lola.

Lola nodded tentatively, and Mr. Hughes carried her on his shoulders as they all walked along the beach. When they got to the release site, the bright yellow sun was just beginning to dip into the horizon. Above it, the sky was a brilliant orange.

They all stopped to stare at the sunset for a moment or two. Then Carlos began taking the babies from the box. As the turtles' feet gripped the sand and they heard the ocean, they began to race toward the safety of the water.

Robin picked up one of the tiny babies and held it up for Lola to see. "This baby couldn't bite you even if it wanted to. Leatherbacks don't have teeth."

She was hoping for a smile but didn't get one.

Mr. Hughes slipped Lola off his shoulders and set her on her feet. Robin bent over and put the baby turtle on the sand. Just as she did, the turtle toppled over. On its back now, it pawed the air with its legs.

Squirm reached out to set it upright again, but Robin nudged him to leave it. Lola stared at the turtle, her face stricken.

"Can you help him get back on his feet, Lola?" Robin said. "Just put your finger right here, at the edge of the shell, and flick your finger up." She pointed to the spot she wanted Lola to touch.

To her surprise, Lola reached out tentatively and did just that. The turtle flipped back on its feet and ran toward the ocean. Lola followed it all the way to the water and watched as it plunged into the waves.

"Bye-bye, baby turtle," Squirm said.

Lola lifted her arm and waved. "Bye-bye, baby turtle."

When the turtle had disappeared into the waves, Lola trotted back to Carlos and helped him lift out more babies. Mr. Hughes watched, beaming with relief.

Robin stared at them both, happy that they were happy. If only she could handle her own fears as easily.

CHAPTER
SIXTEEN

The next day, Griff, Carlos, and the kids ran around helping the church group gather up their things and get ready to go. Several people gave Robin money to support the turtle sanctuary, and before long, she was walking around with a pocket full of cash and cheques. Were the others getting donations too? She hoped so.

As the group members packed up, many insisted on having their picture taken with Carlos. He was shy at first, but by the end of the day Robin saw him smiling in the middle of various clumps of people who were holding out their cellphones. Often, they waved her and the others in as well, and by the end of the day Robin had smiled so much, her face hurt. She didn't mind. Everyone was promising to post the pictures on Facebook and other social media sites, and that was just the kind of media the sanctuary needed.

Finally, the church group and all their belongings were loaded on the bus, and Carlos, Griff, and the kids stood waving as it pulled away.

Robin felt exhilarated. What a great visit it had been. Nearly everyone in the group had raved about their experience and said they'd tell their friends to visit, so Robin knew more good things were going to come.

Back in the dining area, Carlos started stacking the cash and cheques he'd collected into two piles. Robin and the others added the contents of their own pockets, and the piles got bigger and bigger.

When he was done, he picked up a pile in each hand and thrust his money-gripping fists into the air. He whooped and danced around the room. Zo-Zo spun and twirled around him, just as excited as he was.

"New fence for hatchery, new computer, new stove for kitchen," Carlos called out. Dizzily, he fell against one of the tables.

Griff steadied him. "Careful, Carlos."

Zo-Zo called over to Robin. "Did Lola's dad make a donation? He sure looked happy when she picked up that baby turtle yesterday."

"He said he'd include it when he sends us the reward money," Robin said.

"Oh, yeah!" Squirm said. "The reward money." He looked at Carlos. "There's a thousand bucks more to come." He turned to Robin again. "How many more eggs do we have to collect?"

They all looked over at the big thermometer.

"We're at 917," Zo-Zo said. "We're close."

"We can do it," Robin said. She was going to make sure of it.

Zo-Zo twirled again. "Piece of cake."

"How many days do we have?" Squirm asked.

Robin counted on her fingers then counted again. "Five." She looked at the others, unable to believe it. "We only have five days left?"

"That's all?" Surprised as well, Squirm checked the calendar on the wall by the kitchen. "She's right. Whoa."

Griff shook her head. "We've been so focussed on the church group's visit, we've forgotten about our own."

Carlos sat at the table and began separating the cash into various denominations.

Deep lines appeared on Griff's brow. "We'd better get that money in the bank."

"Have own bank," Carlos said. "Very big bank. Big as beach."

Griff's face paled. "Please don't tell me you're going to bury the money in the sand —"

Carlos looked up at Griff. "Never find."

The lines on Griff's face tangled with concern. "Carlos, a lot of people know we had a group here this week. They'll know we got paid. Not putting that money in a bank is just asking for trouble." She stood up. "I won't sleep a wink until it's in a bank. A *real* bank. With a lock on the door. And a vault inside."

Carlos crossed his stick-thin arms across his chest.

"Why don't we just drive into town now and deposit it," Griff prompted.

Robin stared at her grandmother. Griff didn't insist on many things, but when she did, her determination usually won the day.

"If we go now, we can be back by dinner."

Carlos frowned but said nothing.

"Bad things can happen, Carlos," Robin said. "Do it."

"Yeah, do it," Zo-Zo and Squirm echoed.

Carlos grimaced but nodded.

Looking relieved, Griff turned to the kids. "We should be back in plenty of time to go on patrol, but I want you to wait if we aren't."

"We can't wait," Zo-Zo argued. "Especially now that we don't have the church group helping — we have to make every moment count!"

Griff's voice became stern. "I don't want any of you out on the beach without Carlos and me."

Zo-Zo's face turned defiant. "But —"

"No buts," Griff said.

Zo-Zo gave Robin a commanding look.

Robin shifted her eyes to her grandmother. Griff looked tired. They were all tired. This was no time to push things.

Zo-Zo huffed and stormed off to the dorm.

Robin followed and found Zo-Zo sitting on the bed, her knees pulled tightly to her chest, a wild, rebellious look on her face.

"She can't tell me what to do," Zo-Zo said. "If I want to go on patrol, I'll go on patrol. She's not the boss of me."

Robin stared at Zo-Zo. She didn't know what to say. Zo-Zo wasn't used to restrictions. Her dad almost never gave her any, and when he did, Zo-Zo pushed through them like they were made of tissue paper. Griff didn't make many rules, but when she did, they were as tough as wrought iron.

A few minutes later, Griff appeared in the doorway, her purse under her arm. "Squirm is going to be at Benita's with Marcos until we're back." Her deep-blue eyes moved from Robin to Zo-Zo and back again. "So, no beach walking until I'm back. Promise?"

Robin nodded. It didn't really matter if they went out on patrol late, as long as they got out there. Hopefully, her grandmother would be back in time for them to do *some* patrol.

Griff kissed them both on the cheek, waved, and a few minutes later, there was the sound of the van heading off.

Robin spent the next hour at the computer checking messages. People in the church group were starting to post things on their Facebook pages, and the turtle sanctuary now had over a dozen likes. Robin was reading them to Zo-Zo when she got a text.

"It's from Griff," she said aloud.

Zo-Zo leaned her chair away so it was teetering on its back legs. "What'd she say?"

"The van broke down. Carlos is getting someone to help, but she says they're going to be late. Really late. She doesn't want us going out on patrol at all."

Zo-Zo shot forward. The legs of the chair banged on the wooden floor. "I don't care what she says. I'm going on patrol. We need every egg we can get."

Robin felt an arrow of fear shoot through the centre of her chest.

"If we go now, we'll be back before she is," Zo-Zo said. "She won't even know."

"But we promised —"

"*You* promised," Zo-Zo said.

Robin sighed. She had. She wished now that she hadn't.

Zo-Zo sighed too. "I wish adults wouldn't do that. Make kids promise." Her face hardened. "But that doesn't mean we have to do what she says. Griff doesn't know everything. She told us not to chain ourselves to the barn, remember? But if we hadn't done that, the sheriff would have taken the animals!

"And she told us not to go near the factory farm either, remember? And not to do the things we did with the whales." Zo-Zo shook her head. "It's like adults *have* to say no to stuff like that — it's their job! But it's a kid's job to do stuff anyway."

It sounded so logical, so reasonable, Robin thought.

Zo-Zo stood up. "Come on. We'll just go a kilometre or so up the beach, get any eggs that are out there, and come back."

Robin could feel the blood pounding in her chest. It was as if every beat of her heart was shouting, *NO. NO. NO.*

At the doorway, Zo-Zo turned. "Come on, Robs. Don't be a wuss."

Wuss? No way. Robin stood up and followed Zo-Zo out into the darkness.

CHAPTER
SEVENTEEN

From the moment Robin stepped onto the beach, things didn't feel right. She thought for a moment that she had put on someone else's shoes, but knew she was wearing the same ones she'd worn all day. It was weird.

She trudged on. The wind was warm but strong and blasted against her so forcefully that she had to push against it to make any headway. Determined to follow Zo-Zo, she dug her feet into the sand to gain traction, but the ground seemed to crumble with each step.

She exerted herself more, telling herself everything was okay, nothing bad was going to happen. Her body refused to believe her. Her palms were sweating, her muscles were jumpy, and her bowels felt loose, as if they wanted to dump everything. That was scary in itself.

As she moved forward, she tried to convince herself that she was doing the right thing, but each step felt uncomfortable and wrong. It was as if everything inside her was shouting, *Get off the beach!*

Suddenly, she knew she should turn around and go back. This knowing didn't come from thoughts in her head. In fact, her thoughts were doing everything they could to get her stay on the beach, including telling her she was being nonsensical and stupid. What was the big deal about helping Zo-Zo collect eggs?

But there was a growing certainty inside her that couldn't be touched by her thoughts, and this certainty wouldn't go away. Then, as if to make it impossible to ignore anymore, she heard her mother's voice.

Go back, Robin.

Robin stopped walking.

That was when she saw the men.

Two dark figures were running toward them. Robin could tell from the way they were moving, fast and determined, that they were coming for her and Zo-Zo. And that they were dangerous.

"*Run!*" she screamed.

Both of them broke into a sprint.

Robin raced forward, pumping her legs up and down, up and down, with all the strength she had. Feet thudded behind her. Heavy. Pounding. There was the harsh sound of grabbed-for breath. Someone was close, very close. A hand clenched her arm.

Fiercely, she yanked herself free, but the force of the movement pitched her off balance, and she buckled and fell, smashing into the beach. Sand jabbed into her face, and blood burst from her lower lip. She spat and tried to scramble up, but one of the men seized her arm again and, in an iron grip, dragged her into the bushes. A van was parked there, its two rear doors open. The man threw her inside and slammed the doors shut.

She shouted and shouted. A heavy cloth bag was pulled over her head. In complete darkness now, the man tied her wrists and legs, then gagged her. The gag made her lip bleed all the more, and she swallowed blood.

There was a commotion. Zo-Zo was banging on the doors, screaming. "Don't you touch her, don't you —"

The doors opened again, and Zo-Zo was thrown into the van beside her. Robin could hear Zo-Zo's ferocious grunts and groans as she fought the men. But eventually she lay still, and Robin knew Zo-Zo was bound and gagged just like she was.

The van doors slammed shut and the engine started. Robin and Zo-Zo lay on the metal floor.

Kidnapped.

CHAPTER EIGHTEEN

Fear shook Robin awake. She tried to open her eyes, but something tight was wrapped around her head, holding her eyes shut. A blindfold. She lifted an arm to pull it off, but both of her arms moved. Then she remembered. Her arms were crossed and tied together at the wrist in front of her. Her legs were tied too. She swallowed hard and tasted blood from where the gag was digging into the cut on her bottom lip.

The events of the previous night came crashing down on her. She'd been kidnapped. *Kidnapped!* And now she was tied up, lying on what felt like a mattress. She bent her knees, and her skin touched warm flesh. Zo-Zo. Relief washed over her to have her friend close. She wasn't going to have to endure this terrible situation by herself.

Not being able to see, she couldn't look around the room to find out if she and Zo-Zo were alone. What if the men who had captured them were in the room? She didn't sense the presence of others, but maybe they were sleeping. And if they were, she didn't want to wake them.

Who were the men? It had been too dark when she'd been grabbed to see either of their faces. Was one of them Diego? Had he figured out that Robin had told on him? If so, was he going to punish her now? Yell at her? Beat her up? Zo-Zo too?

Even though the room was hot, she felt cold. And desperate.

Think, she told herself. *THINK!*

She tried to calculate how long the van had driven last night before stopping. Twenty minutes? Thirty minutes? It had seemed like forever, but she guessed it had been about half an hour. That meant they were quite a distance from the turtle sanctuary. But in what direction? She had no idea.

Because of the blindfold, she wasn't sure if it was day or night. She sensed it was early morning, but she was so confused and disoriented, it was hard to tell. The only thing she knew for sure was that the room stank of fish. Dead fish. The putrid aroma permeated the air around her and made it hard to breathe.

Ouch! Something bit her leg. She whacked her hands toward it and attempted to hit whatever insect was on her thigh. Whether or not she managed to kill it, she had no idea. She lay still, listening for sounds. A few minutes later, she heard a car going by. Did that mean they were near a town? She listened for more sounds of traffic, but there were none.

Slowly, quietly, she began to move her arms. Even though her hands were bound, she found she could stretch her arms up over her head. She arched and reached back as far as she could. Her hands touched a floor, a dirt floor.

Now something was crawling along her toes. An ant? Or something worse? Were there any poisonous bugs in here? She swished her feet against the mattress and got the insect off, but moments later she felt something on the back of her shoulder. She yanked her arms around, but the way she was tied up restricted her movement. Helplessly, she was forced to lie there while the bug bit her.

Yeow!

Beside her she could hear Zo-Zo swatting bugs as well. Instinctively, they leaned their backs against each other so their bodies were less exposed. Feeling Zo-Zo's back like this calmed her.

Exhausted, Robin dozed off but was woken up again when another bug bit her. The place was infested! As awful as this was, there was something else she had to face that was even worse. She had to pee! How was she going to manage that? Because of the blindfold, she couldn't see. And the ties around her wrists and ankles made it difficult to move. Panic ransacked her, turning her stomach upside down.

Beside her, Zo-Zo began squirming around on the mattress. In a few moments, Robin felt Zo-Zo's fingers at the back of her neck. They began to fumble with the knot on Robin's blindfold. Robin could feel Zo-Zo's hot breath on her skin and tried to stay still.

A long time passed. Robin's need to pee became stronger and stronger. She squeezed her legs together hard.

Suddenly, Zo-Zo's efforts succeeded and the blindfold fell away. Robin's eyes flew open. She scanned the room. The light was dim because there were no windows, but there was enough light coming through the wall slats

to see. There was no sign of the kidnappers. That was
a relief.

The room was small and made of weathered wood,
like an old shed. There was little in the room, just the
bare mattress they were lying on and a pile of fishing nets
piled in one corner. So that's what reeked!

On the far side of the room, two steps led up to a
door. What was on the other side of that door? The rest
of the house? The kidnappers?

Robin eyed the door worriedly. At some point it was
going to open. And when it did? Apprehension tightened
her gut.

Zo-Zo nudged her fiercely, and Robin realized Zo-Zo
wanted *her* blindfold off now. They both shimmied
around on the mattress until Robin was in a good position to work at it. As she tugged and pulled, the tips of
her fingers stung. She had chewed her nails to the nubs
last night, and it hurt to dig them into the cloth of the
blindfold, but she dug them in anyway.

Zo-Zo sighed impatiently.

Slowly, as Robin worked at the knot, the cloth
became more pliable. When it started to loosen, Zo-Zo
yanked her head back and out of it. The moment she
was free, she cranked her head around and they looked
at each other, completely stunned.

Robin stared at Zo-Zo with alarm. Something was
wrong. Very wrong. As she stared at Zo-Zo's face and
looked directly into her friend's eyes, she realized what
it was. Zo-Zo's glasses were gone!

Zo-Zo's tied hands flew up to her face. Her fingers
fumbled for the glasses that were not there. She let out

an agonized groan, then scurried around on her knees and desperately began searching the room, her face just a few inches from the dirt floor.

Robin wanted to help her search, but knew if she moved around, she'd be unable to stop herself from peeing. The urge was so pressing now that she had to wiggle to contain herself.

Zo-Zo reached her arms as far under the mattress as she could just in case the glasses had somehow gotten pushed underneath, but came up empty handed. Frustrated, she jerked her hands up and tried to pull off the gag around her mouth, but it was too tight. She turned to Robin, motioning her to try and untie it, but Robin wasn't able to get it to loosen.

There was a noise behind the door. Robin and Zo-Zo froze. They riveted their eyes on the handle of the door and watched it slowly turn. Then the door opened. A man appeared.

Diego.

CHAPTER
NINETEEN

Diego seemed huge as he loomed in the doorway. The twisted skin of his scar still ruined his neck. His arms were meaty and muscular, and he was holding a sawed-off stick in one hand. He slapped it hard against his open palm and it made a loud smacking sound.

Another man appeared behind him. He was smaller than Diego and had dead eyes. He also carried a stick.

Diego said something in Spanish to Dead Eyes. His tone was harsh, and Robin got the sense that Diego was chewing him out for not tying the blindfolds tight enough.

Diego poked Robin's foot with the stick and motioned for her to get up. Keeping well away from her, as if she were some sort of venomous snake that might shoot forward and bite him, he prodded her again.

Robin didn't move. The rank aroma of cigarettes and alcohol exuded from him. Where was he going to take her? What was he going to do?

Diego shouted at her in Spanish. She stared at him, her body rigid. She'd never been so scared in her life.

Diego put his hands in front of his groin and mimicked the act of peeing. The other man, Dead Eyes, laughed.

Realizing that she was being offered a chance to go to the bathroom, Robin pulled herself to standing. If she didn't go in the next half minute, she'd pee in her pants, and she didn't want that humiliation.

Pressing the wooden club against her front to keep her at a distance, Diego nodded to Dead Eyes, who checked the knots on her hands and feet. Satisfied that they were tight, Dead Eyes went up the two steps and motioned for Robin to follow.

Diego jabbed her hard from behind, and Robin hopped up the steps, then hopped into what looked like the main part of the house. She stepped into a small kitchen. Dirty plates were scattered across the counters.

Dead Eyes motioned to a door, and Robin peeked in. It was a bathroom. There was a putrid smell there, and she turned her head to the side, not wanting to breathe it in. Desperate to relieve herself, she shuffled into the tiny room.

The sink was black with grime, the toilet had no seat, and the bowl was urine-stained. Jiggling to hold in her pee, she turned and tried to pull the door shut, but Dead Eyes pushed it slightly open so he could keep an eye on her.

As quickly as her tied arms allowed, she struggled to lower her shorts. The pee began to stream out of her before she had them all the way down. She crouched, trying not to sit on the filthy toilet, but finally just sank down and did her business. It took her forever to manage the toilet paper, but she finally did.

When she shuffled out of the bathroom, Dead Eyes was pacing. He kept the wooden club against her back as she hopped slowly down the steps. Zo-Zo looked up with relief, and Robin shambled back to the mattress and almost fell onto it, grateful to be alive and unhurt.

From the look on Zo-Zo's face, she knew her friend had been worried sick the whole time she'd been gone.

Diego prodded Zo-Zo and began to take her through the same routine. She made a grunt of protest but stood and hopped up the steps.

When Zo-Zo was back and they were both on the mattress again, Dead Eyes went out and returned with a sack that he tossed into the middle of the room. Robin could see bananas and other fruits sticking out of it. How were they going to eat with gags on their mouths?

Diego was obviously considering this as well. He made a "V" out of two fingers and jabbed them toward his eyes. The message was clear. *Look at me now!* Then he flapped his fingers against his thumb in a talking gesture and slashed his other hand across his throat. It wasn't hard to figure out what he meant: *Scream and I'll hurt you.*

He untied Robin's gag, then Zo-Zo's.

"My glasses! I need my glasses, I —" Zo-Zo's voice was demanding and indignant.

The men looked at her like she was asking for a piece of cake. They turned and left.

Robin was flooded with relief that the men had gone. She didn't know what she'd been expecting, but it hadn't been good.

Zo-Zo threw herself down on all fours again and began searching for her glasses once more.

"They must have come off when they grabbed you on the beach," Robin said.

Zo-Zo blinked, rubbed her eyes, and blinked again. "Everything's so blurry."

Robin leaned against the back wall and tried to clear her mind. She had to think, but she felt too scattered. The inside of her head felt like a hornet's nest that had just been hit with a rock.

She stared at Zo-Zo. Without the barrier of her glasses, she looked so vulnerable.

Zo-Zo slid her index fingers along her eyelids and looked out into the room again. Her face looked hard and determined. "We've got to get out of here."

Robin scanned the room. There were no windows and only one door, the one they had just walked through.

"The only way out is through that door," she whispered hoarsely. "And Diego and Dead Eyes are on the other side of it." There was no way they could overpower two grown men. Besides, she was sure Griff would be coming to rescue them. She said that to Zo-Zo.

"Griff is probably at the police station right now," she said. "She'll launch a search party. Do whatever it takes to find us. We just have to wait until she can resc—"

"That could take days. Weeks! I want to get *out* of here *NOW*!" Zo-Zo picked up a banana and yanked the skin off with her teeth. "I think we should jump them and get the heck out of here."

Robin pulled her bent knees to her chest and wrapped her arms around them. She didn't want to mess with people as brutal as Diego and Dead Eyes. Men who would think nothing of hurting two young girls.

Zo-Zo ate more of the banana. Robin watched her. How could she eat right now?

Robin smacked a bug on her arm. Zo-Zo tried to hit one on her leg.

"We're getting eaten alive," Zo-Zo said. She held out her arms. They were dotted with red bites.

Hearing the men talking in the kitchen, Robin moved over to the door and pressed her ear against the wood. The men were speaking Spanish quickly, too quickly for her to figure out what they were saying, but Robin noticed they repeated one phrase over and over: "*Dos millones.*"

"*Dos* means 'two,' right?" Robin asked. "And doesn't *millones* mean 'millions'? Why would they be —" The realization grabbed her by the throat and cut off her breath. "Are they talking about —" She hesitated, not wanting to make the possibility more real by saying the word aloud. Zo-Zo said it for her.

"Ransom?" Her eyes looked as if they were going to bug out of her head.

Robin forced her lungs to suck in some air. "They're going to try to ransom us? For two million dollars?"

"Sounds like it."

"Our families don't have that kind of money!" Robin said. What was going to happen when the kidnappers found that out?

"Another reason to get out of here. Fast!" Zo-Zo said fiercely. "I think we should start tracking their movements. Listen for what they do, and when. Maybe we'll be able to hear one of them going out. Then we can jump the other one."

Robin wanted to rip the word *jump* out of Zo-Zo's mouth. Was she crazy?

Zo-Zo carried on. "The guy you call Dead Eyes — it's hard for me to see, but isn't he smaller than Diego? He might be easier to overpower."

Every muscle in Robin's body tightened. The idea of fighting either man was scary. Beyond scary. Tears pooled in her eyes. She felt completely overwhelmed.

"We've got to figure out which is the weaker one," Zo-Zo said.

Robin bristled. "Neither one of them seemed *weak* when they threw us in the van." Suddenly, she was back on the beach again and the men were chasing her. These men were dangerous. *Dangerous!* A flash of heat seared through her, prickling her skin. Words exploded out of her.

"You're talking crazy. *CRAZY!*"

"Listen to me," Zo-Zo said.

"I don't want to listen to you. I shouldn't have listened to you in the first place. If it weren't for you, we wouldn't be in this mess."

Zo-Zo's face contorted with pain and she turned away, facing the wall.

The room became hotter and hotter as the day went on, and Robin, utterly exhausted, found herself sleeping and sleeping. There was nothing to do anyway. Zo-Zo was sleeping as much as she was. Robin was just as glad. She didn't want to talk any more about escaping. That would just make everything worse.

But as she was soon to find out, things were going to get worse anyway.

CHAPTER TWENTY

Day Two of their captivity dawned. When Robin opened her eyes, the room was already hot and sticky. Still in shock from all that had happened, she lay on the mattress like a slug, only moving to swat insects, which she did with fierce aggression. It felt good to hit something.

Beside her, she could hear Zo-Zo bashing bugs as well.

Slap. Whap. Bam.

Robin still felt angry. Although it was hard to admit, she was as upset with herself as she was with Zo-Zo. She was the one who had let herself get talked into going on beach patrol. No one had forced her to go. Why had she done it? Just so Zo-Zo wouldn't think she was a wuss? The whole thing seemed so stupid now. But there was no changing what had happened. She was going to have to live with the consequences. Which she was doing right now. Big time.

She heard a sound at the door and looked up. Diego and Dead Eyes were arriving in the doorway, ready to take the girls through the morning washroom routine.

Robin stood up and hopped up the stairs. She knew what to expect now and didn't wait to be prodded. Zo-Zo went next, and after she came back, the men left them a bag of food, a bucket of water, and a cup and went out.

Robin dipped the cup in the cold water and drank deeply, then Zo-Zo did the same. They both flopped down on the mattress again.

"Maybe it's not such a bad thing that they're going to try and ransom us," Zo-Zo said as she examined her bug bites.

Robin looked at her. Zo-Zo seemed less tense. "Why?"

"If they're going to try to trade us for money, they won't hurt us."

"Good point," Robin said. "If Diego can't get his hands on turtle eggs to sell anymore, he's going to need to get money some other way. Or he won't be able to buy his liquor."

"Two million dollars is a *lot* of liquor," Zo-Zo said. "Hopefully enough to drink himself to death."

They were both quiet. Zo-Zo started counting her bug bites. "Fifteen on the front of my body, now for the ones on my back. How many have I got there?"

Robin lifted Zo-Zo's T-shirt and started counting the angry red bites. "Sixteen."

"That makes thirty-one altogether. Let me count yours." She turned Robin every which way so she didn't miss any spots. "Twenty-eight. I win." She smiled.

Despite herself, Robin smiled too. Zo-Zo always liked competing. But competing for bug bites? Who wanted to win that competition?

"Squirm would love this place," Zo-Zo said. "There's every insect known to man in here."

Once breakfast was over, the long day stretched ahead of them.

Robin found a small stick and drew a mark in the dirt floor. "I'm going to make a mark for every kind of bug I see." Not that she knew the names of them. She didn't. So she tried to commit the details of their appearance to her memory, partly so she could describe them to Squirm once they got out of there, but also because it gave her something to do.

Time dragged on.

"This is *so* boring," Zo-Zo said. Yawning, she picked up the small stick Robin had been using and drew two horizontal lines in the dirt, then criss-crossed them with two other lines.

"Let's play X's and O's." She scratched an X in one of the boxes on the grid and handed the stick over to Robin.

They played all afternoon. Zo-Zo was in the lead the whole time. The score was sixty-five games to fifty by the time they switched to playing Hangman. Then Robin was in the lead.

After that, Robin began to pick bedbugs out of the mattress. She wasn't sure the bugs were actual bedbugs, but they were in the mattress, so she called them that anyway.

"I don't care if it takes me hours," she told Zo-Zo as she squished a bug between her thumb and forefinger. It was bad enough that they had bugs crawling on them during the day, but to have them devouring their skin as they slept was just too much.

Zo-Zo helped for a while, then stopped. "For every one we kill, there's like a gazillion others."

The light was dimming in the room when the men came to give them another pee break and dinner. When the men had gone, Zo-Zo reached for the food bag and pulled it toward her.

"And what's on the menu for dinner? More bananas. What a surprise. Just what we had for breakfast."

Robin went over to the bucket and tried to wash her hands in the water that was left. Her whole body felt grubby, and there was grime on her hands and blood under her fingernails from all the scratching she'd done.

When she went back over to the bed, Zo-Zo offered her a banana. Robin shook her head. She wasn't hungry. And even if she had been, she didn't want another banana.

Zo-Zo was peeling one when she suddenly dropped it and grabbed Robin's shoulder.

"Something's moving." Zo-Zo strained forward. She blinked several times as if trying to get her eyes to work better, then pointed to the corner of the room.

"There. By the fishnet."

Robin followed Zo-Zo's gaze and froze.

A snake. Its yellow eyes stared at her from across the room. Its thin tongue flashed in and out of its mouth like small bolts of lightning.

Up until now, Robin hadn't been afraid of snakes. Her mother's interest in them when she'd been little had always made them an item of curiosity rather than of fear. Besides, over the years at The Wild Place, she'd seen enough of them to know they were usually harmless. In Ontario, there was only one species that was poisonous: the Massassauga rattler. But it would only bite if provoked. The snake she was staring at right now didn't look as if it needed provoking.

Zo-Zo squeezed Robin's arm tightly. "It's a snake, isn't it? Only snakes slither like that."

Robin could hear the anxiety in Zo-Zo's voice.

Zo-Zo didn't wait for Robin to answer. "How big is it?"

"It's not big. Maybe a foot long."

"That's not *big*?" She squeezed Robin's arm harder. "Do you think it's poisonous?"

Robin's throat was dry, so dry, she had to force the words out. "I don't know."

The snake began to move. Zo-Zo stiffened. They both watched as it made its way along the floorboards. It stayed near the back wall and finally disappeared into a crevice behind the fishnets.

"Is it gone?"

Robin dragged her eyes from the hole in the wall. Zo-Zo's face was completely white, and there were little balls of sweat on her forehead.

Zo-Zo's afraid. Truly afraid.

Griff was right. Zo-Zo *did* have fears. At any other time, Robin might have been relieved to hear this. But not now. She was having enough trouble dealing with her own fear, let alone adding Zo-Zo's into the mix.

"Yes, it's gone," Robin whispered.

Zo-Zo let out her breath with a whoosh. Then she dropped her head into her hands. "This is a nightmare."

Robin wasn't going to argue about that.

CHAPTER TWENTY-ONE

On Day Three of their captivity, the routine was the same. Diego and Dead Eyes both came in at first light. Dead Eyes checked the knots around the girls' wrists and ankles, then Diego prodded them, one by one, to the bathroom.

Before they left, Diego put down a bag of fruit, and Dead Eyes brought in a pail of water, plus another pail, which was empty.

Zo-Zo gestured toward the empty pail. "I guess that one is in case we need to relieve ourselves between wash-room breaks."

Robin nodded. *Probably.* She doubted whether she'd use it. Who wanted to have the smell of pee in the room all day? The smell of dead fish was bad enough.

"Is the snake around?" Zo-Zo asked.

Robin scanned the room and shook her head. She couldn't see it. But she could hear the men talking in the main part of the house again, so she moved closer to the door and tried to listen.

The men talked on in their usual way, and although Robin tried to figure out what they were saying, she couldn't.

She was just about to move back to the mattress when she heard a ringing sound. A cellphone? Yes, she was sure of it. She pressed her ear hard against the wooden door. The ringing stopped, and Diego, who had a harsher, meaner tone to his voice, started talking in an animated way.

Robin's hopes soared. Maybe he was arranging the ransom. Maybe he was even talking to Griff. Or Carlos.

Diego talked for a while, then all was quiet again.

Robin felt her mood plummet. *But it doesn't matter,* she told herself. Whether Diego was arranging the ransom or not, they were going to be rescued soon. It would have taken Griff a day or so to get the rescue effort going, but once she did, things would move quickly. Griff would *make* things move quickly. Robin was sure of that. Her grandmother would be doing everything humanly possible to find them. Which meant that their rescue should be happening any day now. Any moment. She pictured Griff and Carlos storming through the door.

Please. Come today. Please.

She returned to the mattress, closed her eyes, and tried to figure out what the first sound would be of Griff and Carlos arriving. Would she hear a vehicle pulling up? A shout? A pounding on a door?

Hour after hour, Robin waited for one of these sounds, but none occurred. The sound she did hear was the rustle of Zo-Zo rummaging around in the food bag. Robin sat up.

"Bananas, bananas, bananas," Zo-Zo said. "What I'd give for a piece of pizza. With lots of cheese. And hot peppers." She shut her eyes as if she were in the ecstasy of eating it.

Robin didn't yearn for something hot; her craving was for something cold. Very cold.

"I want ice cream," she said to Zo-Zo. "Maple walnut. When we get out of here, I'm going to eat some every day for a week. No, for a month."

Zo-Zo licked her lips. "Yeah, ice cream. I remember ice cream." She winced and slapped hard at her thigh, but the insect flew off. "These bugs must think *we're* ice cream." She let out a frustrated sigh. "You'd think that stupid snake would eat the bugs."

"It probably does," Robin said.

"Is it around now?"

Robin scanned the room. Ever since they'd first seen the snake, an hour hadn't gone by without Zo-Zo asking where it was. She was beginning to think Zo-Zo was more frightened of the snake than she was of their kidnappers.

"I keep thinking it's going to come for me, and I won't see it until it's too late," Zo-Zo said.

Robin tried to reassure her. "I'll see it."

"Not if you're sleeping."

Robin shrugged. "How do you know it won't bite me and not you?"

"It'll bite me because I'm scared of it."

Robin stared at Zo-Zo. She was even admitting to being scared now. That was a first. But it wasn't necessarily a good thing. Zo-Zo was right. Animals, reptiles included, could sense fear. They knew fear made things weak. That's why they targeted the fearful. They knew weak things couldn't fight back as well as strong things.

Not wanting to think about fear anymore, she drew more grid lines on the dirt floor, put an *X* in one of them, and passed the sick to Zo-Zo. Game after game, Zo-Zo won. Robin didn't really care. She just wanted to pass the time until they were rescued.

When they got bored of playing, Zo-Zo asked her to count bug bites. It was becoming a daily ritual.

Zo-Zo held out her arms. "I have a million."

Robin stared at the bloody and inflamed bites.

"You've got to stop scratching. They're going to get infected, if they aren't already."

"I can't stop myself," Zo-Zo cried. "They're driving me crazy."

Robin finished her count. "Fifty-two." Yesterday, on Day Two, there had been only thirty-one.

"Just fifty-two? Feels like fifty-two *thousand*. Your turn now." Zo-Zo lifted Robin's arms up and started counting. Suddenly, she stopped and became rigid. "Is that him moving over there?"

Robin checked the far wall and saw the snake watching them.

"He freaks me out," Zo-Zo said, barely moving her lips.

"I'm sure if we just leave him alone, he'll leave us alone." Even as Robin said this, she knew it was more of a hope than anything else.

"I think we should kill it."

Robin felt her spine go prickly. If anything was going to make the snake aggressive, it was someone going after it. Zo-Zo wasn't thinking straight. It was just as Griff had said when Lola had visited. People didn't think straight when they were afraid.

"Even if we wanted to kill it, which I don't, we have nothing to kill it with," Robin said, hoping that was going to be the end of it. She hated the idea of hurting anything that lived and breathed. Except insects. She made an exception for insects.

Zo-Zo shrugged, ate half a banana, and lay down again. The room was hot, and in minutes Robin saw that Zo-Zo had fallen asleep.

Quietly, Robin took the remaining piece of banana and shuffled over to where the snake had been. The piece of banana she'd left yesterday was gone. She couldn't be sure the snake had eaten it and not a mouse or rat or other rodent, but she hoped it had. If the snake was feeling full, it might be less likely to go after her or Zo-Zo.

"What are you doing?" Zo-Zo rose on one elbow.

Robin spun around. "J-just looking around. I thought you were asleep."

"I'm *not* asleep." Zo-Zo collapsed on the mattress again. "I *hate* it here. I want to escape."

Robin groaned inside. She did *not* want to talk about jumping the men again. "Maybe we should dig a tunnel. Like in that movie. What was it called?" She moved back to the mattress and lay down.

"*The Great Escape*." Zo-Zo's voice was flat and lifeless. "Yeah, right. They had things to dig with."

Robin yawned. Her eyelids felt as heavy as manhole covers. She couldn't stop them from closing, nor did she want to. Sleeping was the only way she had to get a break from what was happening.

She was nodding off when Zo-Zo spoke again.

"I think we should carry on with our original plan."

Robin forced her eyes open. She swung them over to Zo-Zo. *What original plan?*

"We've been tracking these guys for three days. After they come in the morning, they talk for a bit, then we don't hear a peep out of them until later in the day. I think they leave one guy on watch and the other one takes off for the day."

Robin tried to keep her voice calm. "You don't know that. Just because they're quiet doesn't mean they're not in the house."

Zo-Zo continued as if Robin hadn't spoken. "Next time it's quiet up there, I think we should start shouting. Act like there's a problem or something. They'll come and investigate. If only one of them comes in, we can jump him. And make a run for it."

"A run for it?" Robin held up her legs, still tied together. They couldn't make a run for it even if they wanted to.

"I can hop pretty fast," Zo-Zo said. "All we have to do is get outside. And start screaming. People will come. And help us."

Zo-Zo was talking crazy again. *What people?*

Robin tried to control the riot of emotions that was breaking out in her body. It was as if all her cells were starting to run in different directions, like ants under an overturned rock.

Robin let her head fall back against the wall. A hot sigh burned through her throat. She had to make Zo-Zo realize how stupid this was. But how?

"If there *are* people nearby, they're probably friends of Diego's. Or Dead Eyes's. Why would they help us?"

Zo-Zo rolled her eyes in exasperation. "You shoot down every idea I have."

"I do not."

"Yes, you *do!*"

Robin could hear her own voice rising. "If we jump one of the men and the other one is here, he'll come running in and we'll get beaten to a pulp." She paused. "As you said, they won't kill us because they need us alive, but they'll do everything short of killing us."

"I *HAVE* to get out of here," Zo-Zo said.

Alarmed by Zo-Zo's tone, Robin stared at her face. It looked wild, frenzied.

"I think we should just do it," Zo-Zo said. "Screw the consequences." She stared back at Robin, her eyes full of desperate insistence. An insistence that usually got Robin doing what Zo-Zo wanted her to do.

But Robin didn't *want* to do what Zo-Zo wanted her to do. In fact, she was vehemently against it. The problem was how was she going to stand up to Zo-Zo and refuse?

Trying to buy herself some time, Robin said, "Let's give it another day. Maybe Griff and Carlos will come, maybe —"

Zo-Zo spat out a hot breath. "They'll never come. They'll never be able to find us."

"One more day. Please."

Zo-Zo scowled. "Okay. One more day. But then there's nothing you can do to stop me. I'm going to jump one of them. Or both. And make a break for it."

CHAPTER TWENTY-TWO

Day Four arrived. They'd now been in captivity for three whole days and three whole nights. Before even opening her eyes, Robin said a little prayer. She used the same words she'd spoken every morning, but this time, they were loaded with even more desperation.

Please, please, come today.

She whispered the words quietly inside herself, but even so, her hope was as dead as all the insect carcasses strewn around them. Was Zo-Zo right? That Griff wouldn't be able to find them? She had only one day to do it, or else Zo-Zo was going to take things into her own hands. And if she did that, the outcome would be disastrous. Robin knew that in her head, and she knew that in her gut. But what did it matter? She couldn't figure out any way of stopping Zo-Zo. And if she didn't, bad things were going to happen.

Robin lay on the mattress feeling heavy and immobilized. Zo-Zo seemed as depressed as she was. When the men brought the bag of food, she didn't touch any of it and kept her face to the wall.

The heat was oppressive, and Robin found herself sleeping most of the day. She was glad for sleep. Sleep brought dreams, and in her dreams she found some relief from her awful circumstances. In one dream, she was lying on her bed at home, snuggling Relentless, and in another she was swimming in the cool lake by the farmhouse. If only one of them could have been real.

The dreams were in such sharp contrast to what was on offer in her bug-infested world that she was glad to release herself to them. When she wasn't sleeping, she let herself daydream. The daydreams weren't as satisfying as the night dreams, because part of her stayed aware of her captive reality, but if she let her imagination fly, they could appear to be very real as well. The good thing about daydreams was that she could direct them at will and take herself to imaginary places that contained a few shreds of happiness.

Since food was the easiest thing to have fantasies about, she started her imaginings today with herself crunching down on one of Griff's chocolate-chip cookies. Then she sipped some iced tea. It was cold and sweet, so cold and sweet that she could follow it all the way down her throat to her stomach.

As lovely as these food imaginings were, they did little to satisfy her craving for connection with those she loved. Aching with loneliness, she went off in search of her family. She pictured herself tethered by an extendable cord that was somehow attached to her belly, then floated up and out of the room. First she went to see Squirm. He was hunched over a map and looking more serious than she'd ever seen him.

Then she went to Griff.

She could feel her grandmother's turmoil and angst, see the tortured look on her face as she rushed about, her big hands moving in the air as if she was directing traffic. Poor Griff. She looked miserable. Robin went on to visit her dad and Ari. They too looked devastated. No wonder. They would all be frantic about the kidnapping. It was heartening and frightening to see them all so churned up. But how could it be otherwise?

Again, she whispered to them. *Please. Find us. Come and get us. We're waiting. And waiting.*

She missed them all so much. But there was one person she missed more than everyone else. Someone she'd been missing for a long time. Her mother. She yearned to go to her mother, but was afraid. Afraid that she wouldn't be able to remember her well enough or to feel her close. But as she began thinking of some old memories, walks she used to take with her mother in the woods, talks they used to have over breakfast sometimes, her mother became more and more vivid. Then, suddenly, she appeared, as if in real life.

Robin gasped at the sight of her. Her mother's eyes were bright and her skin was pink and glowing. It was as if she'd never been sick. Overcome by emotion, Robin fell into her arms. Her mother laughed and hugged her tightly. Then the two of them just looked at each other, her mother smiling radiantly. Her smile was like a living thing that moved through Robin's body, easing the terrible tension that gripped her. When she spoke, her voice was warm and reassuring.

"Griff is on her way, my little bird. With your dad. Don't you worry."

They were coming? Did she dare believe that? Hot tears sprang to her eyes. *How could Dad be here in Costa Rica? Did he fly here when he heard the news of the kidnapping?*

Her mother seemed to hear her thoughts. "Yes," she said softly. "Yes, he did."

A lovely rejuvenating warmth swelled into Robin's chest, releasing an avalanche of words. Words that described the turtles, and the eggs, and the sanctuary, words that explained how Zo-Zo had called her a wuss so she'd go on patrol that last night, and finally, words that told her mother about Zo-Zo's intention to jump the men and Robin's terror that she'd actually do it.

"She's going to jump them in the morning. She'll be really mad at me if I don't do it too. I don't know whether to —"

Her mother looked at her tenderly. *I think you do know.*

Did she? Robin closed her eyes. To her surprise, she found a gathering resolve inside herself. Maybe it was because she could feel her mother's strength for the first time in a long while, but suddenly she felt completely and utterly clear: there was no way she was going to do anything that wasn't right for her. No matter how afraid of the consequences she was.

"But how will I … what can I do to st—"

Her mother hushed her. "You'll know what you need to do when it's time to do it. I'll be there to help."

CHAPTER
TWENTY-THREE

Day Five. Robin could tell from the dim light coming in through the slats of wood in the shed that it was almost dawn. This was the day Zo-Zo was going to jump one or both of the men. Robin's whole body cringed at the thought of it.

Not wanting to face the day, she tried to go back to sleep. All she wanted was to be with her mother again, but the dream, in all its loveliness, had disappeared, and she couldn't get it to come back.

Despite that, however, her mother still seemed to be around somehow. Robin wasn't sure how that was possible, but she felt like she used to when she was little and in her own bed alone, aware that even though she couldn't see her mother, she was not far away. The feeling of that was deeply fortifying.

She rolled onto her side. Zo-Zo was lying on her back on the mattress, her eyes wide open.

"I saw my mother," Robin whispered. The words sounded loud in the darkness. They seemed to glow somehow. Like candles in a window on a dark night. "She says Griff's coming."

Zo-Zo let out a long, raspy breath. "You've been saying that about Griff for days."

Robin felt her elation wobble, like a tower of blocks that had been stacked too high. "But this is different, this —"

Zo-Zo cut her off. "It was a dream, Robin. A stupid dream." She turned and looked directly into Robin's eyes. "This is it. Do or Die Day." Her eyes pressed hard into Robin's. "You've got to help. You've got to jump one of them."

Robin felt her desperation rise. *No*, she wanted to scream. *No!*

But if she didn't help, what then? Zo-Zo would be furious with her. She also might escape, leaving Robin alone with both Diego and Dead Eyes. They would take their anger out on her. Would they break her bones? Knock her teeth out? Scar her for life? Robin shuddered.

The room was getting lighter and lighter, and as it did, Robin's apprehension grew. Tension pulled the muscles in her back and neck into tight wires. She started to cry. She wanted her mother and she wanted her now.

There was a sound at the top of the steps. Slowly, the door opened and Diego appeared. In one hand he had the sack of food and in the other he had his prodding stick.

Robin waited for Dead Eyes to come into view behind Diego, but he didn't. Diego was alone. Robin felt an awful certainty pool in her gut. There would be no stopping Zo-Zo now.

Diego started down the steps. His foot landed on the dirt floor.

Robin eyed Zo-Zo. She was getting ready to pounce. The second she started to leap forward, Robin grabbed her arm.

"Don't! Don't do it!"

Alarmed, Diego raised his prodding stick in defence. Just as he was about to smash it down on Zo-Zo's head, the snake shot out of the tangled fishnets.

The snake hurtled through the air like the lash of a whip. Its fangs dug into Diego's thigh, and he screamed in pain, then collapsed to the ground, rocking back and forth and moaning.

Its venom delivered, the snake slithered back into the safety of the nets.

Dead Eyes ran into the room.

"*Serpiente!*" Diego pointed frantically at the snake and tried to get up, but his legs didn't seem to work. He reached his arm out and tried to grab hold of Dead Eyes for help, but Dead Eyes, desperate not to be bitten as well, yanked his arm away and ran out of the room, leaving Diego groaning on the floor.

Seizing the moment, Robin hopped as quickly as she could into the house. Zo-Zo was right behind her. The moment they were through the door, Robin slammed it shut and locked it. Then, seeing a cellphone on the kitchen counter, she picked it up. With her arms still tied, she couldn't hold it and work it at the same time, so Zo-Zo held it while Robin put in Griff's number.

Zo-Zo held the phone between their two heads so they could both hear. Griff answered on the first ring.

Emotion ripped at Robin's chest and throat. "Griff. It's … it's us, we —"

"Oh! My sweet girl, I —"

Her dad came on the phone.

"Robin! Thank God! Where are you?"

"*Dad*!" It was just as her mother had said. Her dad was here! *Here!* Relief overwhelmed her.

"Don't try to talk," he said. "The police will track your location from the phone. We'll be right there."

Robin sat on the front steps with Zo-Zo. Within the hour, Griff, Carlos, her dad, Squirm, and more policemen than she'd ever seen before pulled up in front of the house.

CHAPTER
TWENTY-FOUR

A warm, gentle breeze plump with moisture blew in from the ocean, and a round-faced moon illuminated the beach as they walked along the sand.

Robin had her father on one side and Griff on the other. Zo-Zo was between Carlos and her dad. Ever since the kidnapping, the adults had stayed close, never far from either girl's reach. Squirm skipped ahead, telling everyone he was keeping a lookout.

Tomorrow they were returning to Canada. *Canada.* Robin couldn't wait. Even though it would be cold there, with snowbanks up to her shoulders perhaps, she was eager for it. In fact, she was hoping they'd arrive to a snowfall. There was something magical about snow, the way it could quieten things, even noisy cities, and make everything look white and round and soft.

For the last few days, she and Zo-Zo had made the most of their release from captivity. They both were eating everything they could get their hands on. Except bananas. Robin didn't think she'd ever eat a banana again.

As much as she was enjoying food, Robin soon

realized that the best part of being out of captivity didn't have anything to do with eating. It had to do with freedom. She'd always taken her freedom for granted before, but the kidnapping experience had shown her how important it was to be able to do what she wanted when she wanted to do it. This was the greatest luxury of all. She understood now, more deeply than ever, what an animal must feel when it is taken out of a cage and released into the wild.

And now here she was, released into the wild herself, walking by the ocean for the last time.

"Are you feeling a bit nervous being on the beach again?" Griff asked.

"A little," Robin said.

"Wouldn't be surprised. A bad thing happened to you out here. But we'll keep putting good memories over the bad ones until the bad ones fade."

Robin smiled. That's what she had done with Lola, so she knew this would work. But even though a bad thing had happened, many good things had happened on this trip too. Overall, it had been amazing. She was still very glad she'd come.

She reached into her pocket and fingered the acorn. It always felt so good to touch it. She could still feel the subtle thrumming inside it. But it seemed to match the thrum in her own body now.

Beside her, Zo-Zo crooned, "I hope we find a nest. It would be so great to find one more. Especially on our last night."

Robin wanted to find one too, not only because she wanted her father to see one — he never had before — but most importantly, because she wanted them to reach their egg-collecting goal.

"How many eggs do we still need to find?" Squirm asked.

"Fifty-one," Carlos said.

"That's just one nest," Zo-Zo said.

Robin could hear the yearning in Zo-Zo's voice. It matched the yearning in her own heart. "Then the sanctuary will get the thousand-dollar reward!"

Squirm ran ahead, his bare feet splashing into the foam of the ocean waves as they slid up the sand.

Robin's dad put his arm around her shoulders. "If you start to get nervous, just remember, both Diego and Dead Eyes are behind bars."

Diego had been taken in right after the police had handcuffed him and escorted him to the hospital, where he'd been treated for snakebite. Dead Eyes had been caught the next day.

Squirm ran back to the group. "Will Diego and that other guy go to jail like forever?"

Carlos shrugged. "Kidnapping serious."

"I don't think either of them will be back on the beach for a long time," Gord said.

"I just hope Diego's sentence includes some sort of addiction counselling," Griff said. "For Marcos's sake." Then she added, "I don't think Diego would be half as dangerous if he stopped drinking."

"I don't know," Zo-Zo said. "I think he's just one dangerous dude." She groaned. "And to think I wanted to jump him."

"You did?" Griff snapped her head toward Zo-Zo. "Why?"

"I had to get out of there," Zo-Zo said.

"Thank heaven you didn't do it," Griff said.

"Don't thank heaven. Thank Robin. She's the one who stopped me. Her and the snake." She punched Robin's shoulder playfully.

Robin smiled. It was the closest thing to an apology she was going to get. Not that she cared.

Squirm took off up the beach again, and Carlos began to run after him. When Zo-Zo and Gord fell behind to look at a shell, Griff linked her arm through Robin's.

"You didn't tell me that part. About standing up to Zo-Zo," Griff said. "Good for you for listening to yourself."

Robin wasn't sure she deserved the praise. "I didn't listen to myself when I went out on patrol."

Griff squeezed her arm. "That's how we learn. We make mistakes, adjust, make more mistakes. At least you didn't go along with Zo-Zo and try to overpower Diego."

"Yeah," Robin said. "I had help with that decision."

"What do you mean?"

"It's going to sound weird, but —" She took a deep breath. "Mom. She came to me. Said I'd know what I needed to do when I needed to do it. And she was right. I did." The memory warmed her. "I guess it was just a dream, but she felt as real as you do right now." Her eyes started to sting.

Griff was quiet for a long while. "Dreams can feel awfully real."

"She told me she was going to help. Then that snake bit Diego. It's all so weird, I —"

"Don't know what to think," Griff said, completing the sentence for her. She was thoughtful for a moment.

"You know, the older I get, the more I'm starting to wonder if death really is the end. Maybe we just drop our bodies and move on. Like a snake drops its skin."

They were both quiet for a while. When Griff spoke again, her voice was soft but clear. "But I do know one thing. Love never dies. Especially great love. Like there was between you and your mother." She paused. "Love like that just wraps itself around you. Like a guardian angel. Protecting you."

Robin felt her heart swelling with happiness. She liked the idea of having a guardian angel. And if that angel was her mother, all the better.

Up ahead, Carlos began shouting for them to come. Robin looked up and saw him waving. They all hurried forward. As they did, Robin saw the leatherback tracks in the wet sand and pointed them out to her dad.

"Wow," he said.

Robin grinned. He sounded like a little kid. Like Squirm. She watched as her father knelt and reverently touched the tracks with his fingers.

They caught up to Carlos just as the leatherback was dropping her eggs. When she was done, they all watched her smooth over the area, then haul her massive body back to the ocean.

Robin peeked at her dad's face. He looked enraptured, just as she had been the first time she'd seen this.

Robin and the others positioned themselves in a circle around the nest and started digging up the eggs. The moon was lighting up the beach, and it wasn't long before Robin saw the white curves of the eggs. They seemed to glow in the moonlight.

Gently, she cleared the sand away from one of the eggs and eased it out. She held it in both hands. She felt as if she were holding the future. She probably was.

They piled the eggs up beside the cavernous hole and counted them together, calling the numbers out loud.

"Forty-six, forty-seven, forty-eight, forty-nine —"

Their voices got more and more excited. "Fifty, fifty-one, fifty-two!"

"We did it!" Robin cried. She clapped her hands in delight, and everyone cheered.

Zo-Zo grabbed Carlos's arm and twirled him around.

Squirm danced a jig. "We even have one extra."

Robin couldn't stop grinning. *A thousand dollars. We've just made a thousand dollars for the sanctuary.* She couldn't wait to get back and email Mr. Hughes.

"Let's get these sweethearts into the hatchery," Griff said and turned her attention to packing the eggs into the special bags.

Jubilant, they headed back. As Robin carried one of the bulging bags of eggs, she was aware that in her arms was a whole new generation of life. A generation that would make a big contribution to the ecosystem of Central America, maybe even the world. Things didn't get more thrilling than that.

Zo-Zo came up beside her. "Well, thanks to us, I think the future of the turtle sanctuary is a sure thing."

Robin nodded. "Mission accomplished."

They grinned at each other and slapped their palms in one last high-five.

Time for their next adventure.

ACKNOWLEDGEMENTS

My deepest gratitude goes to the front-line wildlife rescuers in Canada and around the world. In terms of this book, thank you Christian Díaz Chuquisengo of The Leatherback Trust for helping me understand leatherbacks and life in Costa Rica. Thanks also to Kristin Reid, who works for The Leatherback Trust in California, for linking us up, and to Kathleen Martin, the executive director of the Canadian Sea Turtle Network, for her initial encouragement. Special thanks to Audrey Tournay, former director of the Aspen Valley Wildlife Sanctuary, who helped me understand the daily workings of an animal shelter. Her dedication is an inspiration.

In terms of the nuts and bolts of publishing, huge appreciation to Allister Thompson, who edited this book so well and so quickly, and accolades to all the intrepid gang at Dundurn: Jenny McWha, Kathryn Lane, Laura Boyle, Sheila Douglas, Margaret Bryant, and Beth Bruder for all they have done to make this book and the entire Wild Place Adventure Series a reality. And thanks to Guy

Mullally for writing such a great screenplay based on the series books. See you at the movies!

Writerly gratitude to those who made comments on early drafts of the book: Christine Cowley, Barbara Berson, Janet Gardiner, Caroline Smith, Sharon Jennings of CANSCAIP, Ann Creel, Myra Campbell, Martha Patterson, Lynn Leith, C.J. Marjoribanks, Michelle Adelman, and Rod Govan.

Heartfelt appreciation to Rod, Jason, Martha, Gaile, Lizzie, "T," Linda, Caroline, Anna, and Sallie, for all their love and support. It means so much.

And finally, thanks to the kindred spirits who are dedicated to respecting all living things.